DOWN AND DIRTY

"I've done what you asked," Slocum said. "What now?"

"Why, I take you  he reward."

The bounty hunter ——— Slocum. Slocum jerked his hand about as he held it above his head to keep Wilmer's attention diverted. When Wilmer knelt to pick up his six-shooter, Slocum kicked hard. His toe caught in the leather strap and yanked the saddlebags out from under the six-shooter, sending it skittering toward the pit.

When Wilmer's attention strayed, Slocum acted. A quick step forward and a hard kick sent the bounty hunter flailing to land at the edge of the pit. As Wilmer grabbed for his gun, Slocum kicked him again. Man and six-gun tumbled into the pit.

A loud splash echoed up.

"That settles the question of whether there's water in the pit."

"You cain't leave me down here!" came the bounty hunter's angry shout.

"Why not?" Slocum said to himself.

He never wanted to see the bounty hunter again, but he doubted he would be that lucky . . .

JAKE LOGAN

SLOCUM
AND HOT LEAD

JOVE BOOKS, NEW YORK

THE BERKLEY PUBLISHING GROUP
Published by the Penguin Group
Penguin Group (USA) Inc.
375 Hudson Street, New York, New York 10014, USA
Penguin Group (Canada), 90 Eglinton Avenue East, Suite 700, Toronto, Ontario M4P 2Y3, Canada
(a division of Pearson Penguin Canada Inc.)
Penguin Books Ltd., 80 Strand, London WC2R 0RL, England
Penguin Group Ireland, 25 St. Stephen's Green, Dublin 2, Ireland (a division of Penguin Books Ltd.)
Penguin Group (Australia), 250 Camberwell Road, Camberwell, Victoria 3124, Australia
(a division of Pearson Australia Group Pty. Ltd.)
Penguin Books India Pvt. Ltd., 11 Community Centre, Panchsheel Park, New Delhi—110 017, India
Penguin Group (NZ), 67 Apollo Drive, Mairangi Bay, Auckland 1310, New Zealand
(a division of Pearson New Zealand Ltd.)
Penguin Books (South Africa) (Pty.) Ltd., 24 Sturdee Avenue, Rosebank, Johannesburg 2196,
South Africa

Penguin Books Ltd., Registered Offices: 80 Strand, London WC2R 0RL, England

This is a work of fiction. Names, characters, places, and incidents either are the product of the author's imagination or are used fictitiously, and any resemblance to actual persons, living or dead, business establishments, events, or locales is entirely coincidental.

SLOCUM AND HOT LEAD

A Jove Book / published by arrangement with the author

PRINTING HISTORY
Jove edition / February 2007

Copyright © 2007 by The Berkley Publishing Group.

ISBN: 978-0-515-14253-2

JOVE®
Jove Books are published by The Berkley Publishing Group,
a division of Penguin Group (USA) Inc.,
375 Hudson Street, New York, New York 10014.
JOVE is a registered trademark of Penguin Group (USA) Inc.
The "J" design is a trademark belonging to Penguin Group (USA) Inc.

PRINTED IN THE UNITED STATES OF AMERICA

10 9 8 7 6 5 4 3 2 1

1

John Slocum stared at the empty beer mug on the bar, then looked up from the drying foam to the picture of the naked woman stretching ten feet along the back wall of the saloon. He had seen better artwork. And he had been richer than he was. He looked back at the empty beer mug and licked his chapped lips. He had been on the trail for more than three weeks, making his way up the Jornada del Muerto—the Journey of Death—from Mesilla to Las Vegas, New Mexico, and all he had to show for the trip was a half-dead horse and an empty poke.

"You want another, you pay in advance," the barkeep said harshly. He had seen the look on Slocum's face on other cowboys.

"I shouldn't have gotten into the card game," Slocum said. He knew better than to play faro, but the dealer down in Albuquerque had been pretty enough to make him throw caution to the winds. He had played at her table for more than an hour, winning a little, not losing much at all. He had grown bolder and, he hated to admit it, had wanted to impress her. He had bet far too much on a single hand. Even after almost a week, it was hard for him to shrug off the loss. She had probably cheated him but had been so clever at it, he still wasn't certain.

"That's what they all say. You got the nickel for another beer, gimme. If you don't, clear out and make a space for paying customers." The bartender was more truculent than most. Getting out of the hot New Mexico sun was a pastime for most folks in this sleepy town.

Slocum wanted another beer but didn't have the money.

"Where's a gent go to find a job in these parts?"

The barkeep shook his head. "Ain't any in this saloon. We got more deadbeats talkin' themselves up as bouncers than I can shake a stick at."

The bartender looked at Slocum, at the worn ebony butt of the Colt Navy slung in its cross-draw holster. His eyes flickered up to meet Slocum's cold green eyes, and then went back to the six-shooter.

"You got the look of knowing how to use that."

"That's not the kind of work I'm looking for. I can wrangle with the best, and I'm not afraid of a day's hard work."

"Reckon not," the barkeep said a mite uneasily, still staring at the six-gun. "But there's nothing to keep a man in Las Vegas these days, unless you got something to do with Fort Union. Haulin' supplies there, banking, feedin' or waterin' the soldiers when they come into town. All the ranchin's dried up along with the desert. Worst drought I ever saw, and it's held on for two years already."

"I came up from Mesilla," Slocum said. "There's hardly any water in the Rio Grande anywhere along the way."

"Heard there's plenty up around Taos, but then again they're as hard up as we are here when it comes to decent jobs. Or so I've heard." The barkeep cocked his head and finally said, "You might consider looking on up in Colorado."

"That's the best advice you can give me?" Slocum asked wryly.

"Nope. Best advice is to plunk down two bucks, and I'll

give you a half bottle of whiskey. Drink it, get roarin' drunk, and the world'll look a sight better then."

Slocum patted his vest pocket looking for a coin—any coin. He came up empty.

"Should go make my own luck," he said.

The barkeep grunted, grabbed the empty mug, and gave it a quick swipe with his rag before putting it back on the stack behind the bar. If Slocum wasn't drinking, he wasn't talking anymore.

Slocum left the saloon and looked up and down the main street. Las Vegas was a decent-sized town, but heat had driven everyone indoors for a siesta. He started around the side of the saloon where he had tethered his Appaloosa, but stopped when he saw a stagecoach rattling into town and coming to a halt at the depot across the street. Slocum dropped into a chair, rocked back, then pulled his hat brim down enough to keep it from being obvious he was watching the passengers and driver intently. If he had no prospects for a legitimate job, that left drifting over to the illegal. The sight of the stagecoach suggested there might be a few dollars waiting to be picked from an incautious driver.

Slocum grinned. There wasn't even a shotgun messenger on the stage.

He watched the driver open the door for the three passengers, all dusty and sweaty from their ride from up north. Might be they had come from Denver. They had certainly come from somewhere in Colorado. Two men spotted the saloon and made a beeline across the street, using their sleeves to wipe dust from their lips in preparation for a beer.

"Hope this place has jobs," said the first man, pushing through the doors and going in.

Trailing, his traveling companion said, "I hear you. Been huntin' myself for more 'n a month. Nuthin' in Denver, nuthin' in Raton. Hell, even the freighters aren't hirin'." His words were swallowed by the barkeep's booming voice asking what his two new customers wanted.

Slocum looked back at the stagecoach with renewed interest. There wasn't much point drifting northward, as the barkeep had suggested, if these two were coming south hunting for work. Slocum didn't much understand it, but something had happened back East and the country's entire economy was in the shithouse. The Panic of '73 was continuing all the way into the summer of '74, as he could attest. Railroads failed, and the Grant Administration hadn't done much to put its own house in order. Slocum usually ignored such things, even when the newspapers' bannered headlines foretold doom and disaster, but this time he was affected by the bad times.

With no work and no prospect of work, the unguarded stagecoach looked increasingly tempting. A moment of "Stand and deliver" and he'd be a few dollars ahead. Didn't much matter to him right now if all he got were greenbacks. He had done worse things than being a road agent in his day.

Slocum heaved himself to his feet and walked over to talk with the third passenger, a rail-thin man dressed in a black coat. From the severe cut of the man's clothing and the wild look in his jet black eyes, Slocum thought he might be a hellfire-and-brimstone preacher. In this weather, all the man needed to provide was the brimstone. Hellfire was available just by stepping into the sun.

"Afternoon," Slocum said. "You just came in on the stagecoach."

"I did," the man answered. "Are you with the company?"

"The stage company? Nope, I was wondering about the cargo. It looked like they were riding mighty low, meaning they have quite a cargo although there's only the three of you passengers."

"Payroll," came a cold voice behind Slocum. "The stage

carries the Fort Union payroll from time to time. But not today."

Slocum glanced in the window of the depot and saw the reflection of a man wearing a star. He turned and faced the marshal.

"I'm looking for a job as guard," Slocum said. "If they carry that much money, they might need—"

"They don't need nuthin'," the lawman said. He worked a bit on the tip of a waxed mustache, but as fast as he twirled it, the hot sun melted the wax and made his efforts come to naught. This didn't deter the man, who only toyed with his mustache as a nervous gesture.

Slocum saw the way the marshal's right hand stayed close to his six-shooter, fingertips tapping nervously against the leather holster. That was a bad habit that would get the man killed in a real fight, but Slocum wasn't going to call him out. There was no reason to leave bodies behind when all he wanted was a few dollars to put into his pocket.

Unless the marshal had recognized him from a wanted poster. John Slocum's journey through the West hadn't been pure as the wind-driven snow. Worse than the occasional robbery he had committed, a federal warrant for judge-killing had dogged him all the years since the war. He had returned to Slocum's Stand in Calhoun, Georgia, to farm. His parents were dead and his brother Robert had died during Pickett's Charge. Slocum had not counted on a carpetbagger judge taking a fancy to the farm, or the lien for nonpayment of taxes. It had all been fraudulent, but what wasn't in dispute was the judge's grave on the hill by the springhouse. Slocum had ridden out and never looked back, but the wanted posters had kept circulating until he wondered how any lawman didn't know his face as well as his own.

"They don't need a stranger lookin' after their cargo," the marshal said with an edge to his voice. His finger-tapping sped up and he squared off, as if Slocum would throw down on him.

"Mind if I ask for myself?"

"The soldiers from the fort look after the payroll shipments," the marshal said. "I look after everything else. *Every*thing else."

Slocum stared at the man for a moment and saw he wasn't going to back down.

"You need a deputy?"

The question took the marshal by surprise. His eyes widened, and he started to say something, but the words jumbled up.

"Reckon not," Slocum went on, taking some small satisfaction in momentarily confusing the lawman. It was reckless to make enemies, especially of those who wore badges on their vests, but Slocum wasn't in a mood to bandy words.

"I'd take it as a personal favor if I never saw you around town again," the marshal said, getting his wits back. Slocum wondered if this meant he would rush off to his office and the stacks of yellowed, brittle wanted posters and start leafing through them. Probably not. It was too hot for such dusty work.

"I'll be moving on when it gets a mite cooler to travel."

The lawman nodded once, hitched up his gun belt, and stopped tapping his fingers against his holster.

"See that you do."

Slocum looked to the doorway leading into the adobe depot where a frail man stood. The stagecoach agent coughed and spat, then said, "Don't go gettin' him too riled, son. He's got a mean streak." The man hesitated, then added, "And we don't need no guards. Nothing worth two hoots and a holler ever comes in, 'cept the fort payroll."

"And it's guarded by soldiers," Slocum finished. The man nodded, coughed consumptively, and spat again. There was as much blood as sputum in the gob hitting the edge of the boardwalk. He took a few steps and got closer to Slocum, then peered up myopically. The old man gasped and turned pale under his weathered hide.

"I . . . I got business to tend to," he said, backing away. Slocum wondered at the agent's reaction, but not too much.

Slocum walked back into the hot sun, giving the Concord coach a once-over as he passed. The weight in the rear boot causing it to sag there might have come from a canvas sack of gold coins, or it might have been something else. Whichever it was, Slocum decided it might be interesting to find out.

He looked around as he went back to the shady side of the saloon and paused before he mounted. The marshal and two deputies watched him like hawks from across the street. The marshal turned to one deputy and spoke rapidly. Slocum didn't have to have ears like a rabbit to know what was being said. As long as he was within the marshal's jurisdiction, he would have a human shadow following him around. That posed something of a problem if he wanted to stop the stage and find out what its cargo was firsthand.

He mounted and rode south, the deputy following. Slocum wondered what was happening when the station agent shuffled over to the marshal and began yammering at him, arms waving around like a windmill in a stiff breeze. The marshal and agent were rapidly left behind as Slocum trotted out of town and away from all the intrigues boiling around him. In spite of the heat, he kept a brisk pace as he hunted a spot he remembered in the road on his way into Las Vegas. Tall rocks rose on either side of the road, blocking a clear view farther along. A sudden turn just past those rocks would force a stage to slow, giving an enterprising highwayman the opportunity to hold up the coach.

Slocum rode steadily until he was a couple miles outside town. The deputy finally gave up, thinking his quarry was on the trail for good, heading back to Santa Fe. Finding a shady spot in the midst of robust junipers and a few spindly piñons gave him the chance to water his horse in a small pool and to look around. What he saw didn't suit him or his plans. Everywhere he saw evidence of soldiers camping for extended periods of time. Their bivouac showed large numbers of the bluecoats came here often, maybe to guard their monthly payroll shipment. He knew little of Fort Union other than it was a quartermaster's delight, supplying most of the other forts in the region.

Slocum bent and picked up a corroded brass belt buckle with crossed sabers and US in raised letters prominent on it. He tossed it hard against a tree trunk. It stuck in the wood. He considered drawing and firing at the target, but refrained. He was here to scout a possible ambush point, not to show what he thought of the Federal soldiers.

He poked around another half hour, and decided that he ought to forget the stagecoach robbery and consider it too risky for indeterminate return. Slocum half-believed the marshal when he said that nothing of value was sent on the stage, other than the fort payroll. The entire region was locked in poverty. The best he could do was water his horse, let it graze a mite, fill his canteen, and then ride on hunting for greener pastures.

"Taos," he muttered. That had been the end of the trail for the Bent brothers when they'd run their trading post out of Bent's Fort up in Colorado, near the Kansas border. Prosperity had come to Taos and eventually Santa Fe, but the towns in between like Las Vegas were suffering.

"Hell, for all I know Taos is a dead end too," Slocum grumbled. His Appaloosa looked up, eyes wide at his outburst. He patted the horse's neck, grabbed the reins, and swung into the saddle. The road back to Las Vegas was dusty and seemed longer than when he had ridden out, but the reception he got at the edge of town took him by surprise, even after the marshal's declaration of wanting him permanently gone.

"Reach for that hogleg and I'll blow you in half," the marshal said, a long-barreled shotgun pointed at Slocum.

"Yeah, grab some sky!" piped up the deputy who had followed Slocum out of town earlier.

"What's wrong, Marshal?" Slocum didn't pay any attention to the excitable deputy. The marshal was the one in command, and anything the other lawman said could be safely ignored.

"You're what's wrong," the marshal barked. Slocum saw sweat beaded like fat raindrops on the man's forehead. It was hot, but there was a tremor in the marshal's hand that hadn't been there before. He was a nervous man; the finger-tapping had told Slocum that much. But now the marshal was outright scared. The way his finger was pulled back so far on the shotgun trigger that it turned white made Slocum uneasy.

"No need to get all hot and bothered," Slocum said. "I decided to head for Taos, not Santa Fe, and I have to ride back through—"

"Shut up!" The marshal was getting more nervous by the instant. His deputy was already hopping from foot to foot in excitement as he waved his six-shooter around wildly.

Slocum looked past the marshal and deputy to the doors and windows of Las Vegas's main street. The town had been taking a siesta when he was here hours earlier. Now it appeared that everyone had taken a sudden interest in what went on outside. He saw noses pressed against windows and fingers wrapped around doors, in case they had to be slammed shut. No one looked like they were rooting for Slocum.

"Mind telling me what's got you so riled? I'm not—" Slocum had to force himself not to go for his six-shooter when the marshal discharged his shotgun into the air. The lawman hurriedly knocked out the shell and slammed in a new one. If Slocum had gone for his six-shooter, the deputy would have started flinging lead around. In his agitated state, he wouldn't have been able to hit the broad side of a barn even if he was locked inside, but Slocum wasn't taking a chance the man might get in a lucky shot.

"The jail's over there," the marshal said. "You keep those hands where I can see 'em and ride to the jailhouse."

Slocum did as he was told, puzzling over the lawman's sudden change of outlook about drifters in his town. It cost the town money to put up a prisoner, but nothing for the marshal to chase away the riffraff. Slocum would have thought the marshal was out to collect a fine for some minor infraction, except for the state of nerves he showed.

Slocum dismounted and turned. The deputy grabbed for his Colt. Slocum had an opportunity to grab the frightened man and use him as a shield, but the chance passed as the marshal moved quickly to get a clear shot.

"Inside. Now, move it now!"

Slocum obeyed and found himself facing two cells. A man lounging on the iron cot in one sat up in a hurry and stared at Slocum. His mouth fell open.

"Quit gawking, Murray," the marshal snapped. "You'll catch flies if you leave your mouth open too much."

"Flies're better than the swill you serve as dinner," the prisoner said. Slocum saw the answer was reflexive. The man kept his eyes fixed on Slocum, and the deputy herded Slocum into the other cell and slammed the door so hard the entire cell rang like a bell.

"Be sure you got the door locked this time," the marshal said to his deputy.

"It's locked. Honest. You can check it and see."

"I'll trust you this time," the marshal said. "Get on over to the telegraph office and send the 'gram I wrote up. The federal marshal'll want to hear about what we got."

Slocum puzzled over the marshal's words. He glanced at the posters tacked to the wall, and even peered at a couple on the lawman's desk. None of them showed a charge for judge killing.

"Marshal," the deputy called from the doorway. "You got to come quick. They's bustin' up the saloon again, and I can't handle 'em all myself."

The lawman quickly crossed the small office, grabbed the cell door, and rattled it a few times to be sure Slocum was securely locked inside. No matter what he had told his deputy, he didn't trust him to make fast the iron bar door.

"You behave yourself," the marshal warned, then ran from the jail swinging his shotgun around like an elephant trunk.

Slocum sat on the cot in his cell and tried to puzzle out what was going on. He looked over at the other prisoner, who stared at him.

"What?" Slocum demanded.

"I never figgered a hick-town marshal like him would capture anyone like you, Neale."

"Who's Neale?"

The prisoner laughed nervously. "I got it, Neale. You don't want to fess up who you are."

"Who's Neale?" Slocum repeated.

"Sorry," the man said, sounding as if he meant it. "I won't slip up again."

Slocum heard the unspoken "Neale" tacked onto the end of that sentence. Who the hell was Neale?

2

Slocum paced the tiny cell like a caged animal, but he wasn't working off nervous energy. Every time he made a circuit of the small cell he noticed something new, something different, something that would enable him to bust out of the calaboose. He finally collapsed on the cot and stared hard at the weak point he had discovered. For all the strength of the lock on the cell door, the hinges were poorly constructed and the hinge pins exposed. A little work using the proper tool would cause the door to fall off.

The only problem Slocum saw was the lack of the proper tool.

"What're you so nervy about?" the other prisoner asked. "They got you dead to rights? Gonna ship you out right away? This ain't such a bad place to spend a few days."

"How's the food?" Slocum couldn't have cared less about the grub served up by the marshal. He wanted the prisoner's attention on other things as he ran his fingers under the cot, hunting for the right tool.

Slocum almost cried out in triumph when he found the segment of the cot leg that had come loose. A little prying popped it free from the frame. He hid it from his fellow prisoner, not knowing what the man might say or do at the

12

prospect of an escape attempt. For all Slocum knew, the man was in for some minor crime and would turn Slocum over to the marshal for a quick dismissal of charges against him.

"You plannin' on bustin' out?" the man asked, startling Slocum. Slocum hid the length of metal to keep the other prisoner from seeing it.

"No reason to," Slocum said. "I haven't done anything." This produced a belly laugh.

"You got quite a sense of humor, Neale," the man said. "Sayin' you ain't done nuthin'!"

"What are you locked up for?"

The laughter died as the man sat up on his cot and stared hard at Slocum. "I killed a man in a saloon brawl."

"A fair fight?" Slocum knew the answer by the expression of pure rage on the man's face.

"Yeah, right. Him or me." The prisoner paused a moment, then said, "Look, we got to get out. They'll only hang me. You . . ." He left the sentence dangling, as if there might be something worse than having your neck stretched.

Slocum went to the cell door. He had to trust the other man wouldn't call out. He had no idea if he was locked up for murder or simply being in the wrong place. Las Vegas was the wrong place for more than one of them, if true.

"Whatcha doin'?" the man asked.

"Getting out of here. Keep an eye out for the marshal."

"Hell, if him and his worthless deputy are bustin' up a fight at the saloon, they'll be there all night. Break up the fight, have the house buy 'em drinks. That's the way it works."

"I hope you're right." Slocum grunted as he forced the metal rod up hard against the bottom of the hinge pin. Slocum fell heavily against the bars when the pin popped out easily. He hadn't remembered a squeak as the cell door opened for him and then closed behind him. The marshal was efficient maintaining his jail cells—and it was going to get Slocum out of the hoosegow in a hurry. The second pin popped up with hardly more pressure.

"You're a genius, Neale!" cried the other prisoner. "Get me out. You got to get me out too!"

Slocum gripped the door and lifted a little, pressing outward. He staggered as the door fell off its hinges, and he was left holding its ungainly weight. He slid around the side of the now-open door and then leaned it back against the bars. A quick look at the other prisoner decided him. The man might be a backshooter, but unless Slocum murdered the man where he stood looking so anxious and needy, he would be screaming his head off for the marshal before Slocum got outside.

"Where's the marshal likely to keep the horses? He took mine."

"Corral's out back. He's got my horse there too."

Slocum grabbed the key ring out of the top desk drawer and tossed it to the man, who hastily opened his cell.

"Thanks, Neale. You ever need anybody to watch your back, I'm the one for you."

Slocum rummaged about and found his Colt Navy and tucked it into his cross-draw holster. He peered out the door, and was happy to see that twilight had settled on Las Vegas and cast long shadows everywhere. He stepped outside into shadow and moved to the back of the jailhouse. The other prisoner crowded close behind.

"There, there's the corral. That bay is mine."

"Saddle up and let's ride," Slocum said. He didn't care that the man still thought he was someone named Neale. In return for being released from his cell, he had told Slocum where to find his Appaloosa. That had saved a lot of hunting that might have alerted the lawmen.

Slocum had saddled up and started walking his horse out when the prisoner let out a yelp.

"The marshal! He's gonna find we're gone!" With that

the one-time prisoner let out a whoop, put heels to his horse, and shot from the corral. He had his six-shooter out and blazed away at the marshal as he hit the main street at a dead gallop. The marshal and his deputy responded fast, returning fire and running a few paces after their escaped prisoner.

Slocum drove the two other horses in the corral out after the retreating prisoner, adding to the confusion and making sure it would take the two lawmen a while to get on the trail. Without waiting, Slocum cut along behind the buildings on the main street, cut down a side street, and kept moving until the furor lay far behind him. He glanced up at the stars and got his bearings. Fate or luck had him on the north side of town. It took only a few minutes before he crossed the road to Taos.

He considered the matter for a moment, then set out at a steady clip, wanting to put as much distance between him and Las Vegas as possible. If he read the marshal right, the lawman would go after the other escaped prisoner because he had spotted him and the direction he fled. That gave Slocum more than a decent lead—it might put him in the clear if the marshal and his former prisoner shot it out.

The Milky Way provided almost enough light to make Slocum think he was riding along on a cloudy day, though it was nowhere near as hot as a day would have been. Slocum pulled up his collar and shivered a mite. The mountains furnished a gentle, cool breeze off their heights, and the desert cooled fast once the sun had sunk behind the Sangre de Cristo Mountains to the west. The fresh air filled Slocum's lungs and gave him new resolve. He didn't understand what had gone on back in Las Vegas, and it no longer mattered. He wouldn't return there any time soon, not with the promise of Taos and beyond ahead of him.

He slowed and eventually dismounted to let his horse rest. When he found a watering hole near the road, Slocum considered bedding down for the night. His horse drank, and he filled his canteen with fresh water as he thought on the problem of the Las Vegas marshal and decided to push on as far as he could. The lawman wasn't likely to pursue beyond the limits of his authority, no matter whom he had thought he'd locked in his jailhouse.

"Neale," Slocum said, shaking his head. He had known a Neale or two in his day, but not one worth the response the marshal and his deputy had shown after the station agent had talked with them. One Neale had ridden with Slocum for a few weeks, but Slocum had never considered him to be his partner. His habits had been bad, he ate the damnedest things—armadillo had never set well with Slocum's belly—and his lack of good sense had doomed any chance Slocum might change his opinion. There had been a few other casual acquaintances with that moniker, but none of them was likely to be a lawbreaker. One had been a preacher secure in his faith, and the other had been blinded during the war when his cannon barrel had ruptured, spitting shrapnel into his face.

He rode for another hour. A check on the wheel of stars above showed it to be around midnight. He had been riding steadily for more than four hours and had no sense of anyone from Las Vegas on his trail. Still, Slocum was a cautious man and found a low rise with a good view of his back trail. Using his field glasses and a lot of patience, Slocum watched the empty trail for more than a half hour without seeing any rider.

He led his horse off the trail a ways, found a grassy area, hobbled the horse, and unfurled his bedroll. It took a few minutes for him to dig out rounded cavities in the ground to accommodate his hips and shoulders; then he stretched out on his blanket. Only the usual night sounds reached him, lulling him to sleep within minutes.

Slocum awoke just before dawn at the metallic click of a six-gun cocking.

"Don't go stirrin' yer bones none," came the cold command. "I don't wanna plug you, but I will."

Slocum blinked his sleep-caked eyes, and finally focused on a squat man who looked to be as wide as he was tall sitting on a nearby stump with his six-shooter pointed at him.

"Who're you?" Slocum fought back the drowsiness that still clouded his mind. He tried to remember if he had ever seen the man before, and doubted it. The stench coming from him was overpowering. It was a good thing the man had approached from downwind, or Slocum would have been up and firing before he had gotten within twenty feet. The man wore buckskins that had seen better days years earlier and moccasins patched so many times there was hardly any of the original left. From what Slocum could tell, the man's face fit his body. Thick, brutish, and scarred. His nose had been mashed so many times it was flat and lopsided above a dirty blond mustache. The eyes were hidden under heavy bony ridges, but Slocum had the feeling they never strayed from his quarry.

And the pistol in the man's grimy hand never wavered.

"Ain't important who I am 'cuz I got the gun and you don't."

"Get the hell out of here and let me sleep in peace or shoot me. Right about now, I don't care which," Slocum said.

"Don't want to shoot you, Neale. The reward's bigger if you live to stand trial. Damn shame, I'd say. Better to get a hundred dollars, though, than only twenty-five fer you dead. Don't know why the station agent set it up that way, but he did. Orders from the home office, he said, but I think it was all his doin'."

"Nice to know this Neale is worth more alive than dead," Slocum said. Anger fueled him now and drove away the last of his fatigue. He glanced over to where his Colt dangled in its holster. With the intent look of this bounty hunter, there was no chance he would glance away for even an instant. Slocum stirred and flopped the blanket around him as he reached for the derringer he carried in his vest pocket. His fingers closed on it, and he managed to fumble it out, then dropped it. The man didn't notice in the dark.

"Don't go tryin' to fool me. I know you, Neale. You're gonna swing, trust me. But only after they git done with you."

"I'm not Neale." Slocum flopped the blanket around some more as he pushed it away and retrieved his derringer. He didn't dare try to shoot it out with the man since his small-caliber weapon might not drop the bounty hunter before he loosed a .44 slug into Slocum's head.

But Slocum hid the derringer and felt reassured at its cold metal pressing into his palm. He sat up, faced the bounty hunter, and crossed his legs.

"Don't make no never mind to me what you want to call yerself. You're Neale and that's good enough fer me and the law. They'll fork over the reward so fast, the gold coins might melt."

"Who're you?"

"Name's Wilmer. Reckon you might as well know what varmint caught you so easy." The man spat, his gun hand never wavering an iota. "Fact is, you ain't half as tough as they made out. I've run to earth scoundrels twice as mean and ten times as ugly."

Slocum wasn't sure if he had been insulted, and it didn't matter to him. He still didn't have a good shot at the bounty hunter.

"Nuff of this here jawin'," Wilmer said. The bounty hunter stood and Slocum had to blink in surprise. Wilmer hardly topped five feet tall. When Slocum stood, he towered a full foot above him.

Wilmer let out a low whistle.

"They didn't say you was a giant. Don't matter to me, though—"

"You're the meanest bounty hunter this side of the Rio Grande," Slocum finished for him.

"You got more of a sense of humor than I'd thought you would too."

"That's because you have the wrong man."

"Nope, got the right one. I don't read so good, but pictures, I never forget 'em. I seen you on that poster and it's a damn good likeness."

"What am I wanted for?"

Wilmer never got the chance to answer. He started to laugh and when he did, he moved to hold his ample belly with both hands. Slocum moved faster than a striking rattler, raising the derringer and pointing it squarely at the man's face.

"Drop it or I'll drop you," Slocum said in a tone that brooked no argument.

"You mangy—"

"Now!"

Slocum's finger was drawing back on the trigger in preparation for firing. Wilmer hastily let loose of his pistol. It rolled around the bulge of his belly and tumbled to the ground, hitting a rock and discharging. In reaction Slocum fired, but both the round from the bounty hunter's six-shooter and Slocum's derringer missed hitting anything vital.

Slocum cursed, fired the second barrel, and dived for his Colt. By the time he got it out, Wilmer had hightailed it for the dense undergrowth a few yards away. Slocum heard the bounty hunter thrashing about wildly in the dark, and then nothing. He paused, suddenly wary. Wilmer was no fool. Slocum felt as if the jaws of a bear trap were getting ready to snap shut on his foot. Standing, waiting, listened intently, but heard nothing at all. Wilmer had obviously spent most of his life in the wilderness. He might even have been one of the last mountain men and more at home in these mountains than he would ever be among civilized men.

Slocum retrieved Wilmer's fallen pistol and tucked it into his waistband, then slung his holster around his hips and secured his Colt Navy. Drawing the bounty hunter's six-gun, he took a couple steps in the direction of the woods, then shook his head. He looked around and didn't see another horse. Wilmer had walked up on him without so much as disturbing the chirping of the crickets. Trying to track down the man might be impossible, and he wasn't sure what he would do if he caught up with him. Trying to convince Wilmer that he wasn't this person named Neale was a fool's errand. He wished the bounty hunter had been more talkative about who this Neale was and what he was wanted for. If wanted posters were widespread throughout New Mexico, it was time for Slocum to find cooler pastures, maybe in Colorado.

He quickly rolled up his gear and stowed it on the back of his saddle, then mounted. Another slow survey of the area failed to betray Wilmer's presence, though he could feel the man out there. Wilmer was too good a woodsman for Slocum to know where.

Slocum considered getting on the road for Taos, but veered away, cutting across the mountain meadow and going into the rockier hills. He stood a better chance of covering his trail here than on the road. His Appaloosa strained as he worked his way ever higher into the Sangre de Cristo Mountains. All around he saw abandoned mines, their tailings belched out down the steep slopes. He slowed as he came into wide valleys, aware that ventilation shafts into the mines would likely be grown over and not marked. A miner had other things than safety on his mind—the lure of gold or silver would blind him to anything but digging like a badger and rummaging through massive heaps of rock blasted from the belly of the mountain.

Keeping a careful watch on the ground caused Slocum to stop and look closely at hoofprints cut into the grass. He sat, contemplated what he saw, and finally decided no fewer than six men had ridden this way within the last day. Nothing but abandoned mines told him this was either a posse to be avoided or a band of outlaws intent on avoiding a posse. Lawmen or road agents, it didn't matter. Slocum intended to ride clear of them and the trouble either posed.

He found it difficult to keep that promise to himself because two riders appeared from a stand of aspens not a hundred yards away. The sun was behind Slocum, forcing them to squint into the sun if they looked in his direction. He stood stock-still and waited to see if they spotted him. He heaved a sigh of relief when they kept riding, unaware of his presence. From their appearance, he guessed they weren't lawmen. Whether they were road agents or peace-abiding men only traveling through was something he couldn't tell, but his gut told him they were on the wrong side of the law.

"Just like me," he muttered. A quick thought came to him that one of them might even be the mysterious Neale that both the marshal and bounty hunter wanted so desperately. If he captured this Neale, he might get out from under the cloud of suspicion that was choking him. The thought passed as good sense prevailed. Better to get away from Neale and Las Vegas and Wilmer entirely than to get mixed up in some situation he knew nothing about. It was hard enough fighting his own battles without becoming involved in someone else's.

Slocum walked his horse slowly to the edge of the meadow to keep from attracting attention, then rode more quickly until he found a canyon branching away, more or less in the direction of Taos. An hour later he was feeling good about eluding the riders behind him. The valley he traveled now was dotted with dozens of shafts, and the slopes rising gradually on either side were festooned with holes that had been blasted and dug and abandoned, some fairly recently from the look of the tailings. Slocum angled toward one of the mines, thinking to find a line shack where he could grab a few more hours of sleep and maybe find an airtight or two of food left behind. Peaches or tomatoes would go down mighty fine right now and save him the trouble of bagging a rabbit. In spite of the feeling of solitude, he knew there were at least a half-dozen men roaming these hills.

And Wilmer.

How intent the bounty hunter was on tracking him, Slocum could not say. He hoped chasing the man off the way he had had dampened his enthusiasm for a hundred-dollar bounty—but not to the extent he would shoot Slocum in the back and settle for a quarter of that.

Slocum picked a mine that couldn't have been abandoned more than a few weeks and rode to it, avoiding several open pits. What these had been used for was a puzzlement since it appeared that the shafts were blasted directly into the mountainside. But then miners tended to be as crazy as bedbugs and took it into their heads to do odd things in their search for gold.

He dismounted and went to a shack, opened the door, and looked around inside. The shack had been left almost in the same condition as when some hard-rock miner had lived here. The bed was nothing more than dried grass stuffed into a canvas bag. A rickety table and an even less secure chair were pushed against the far side of the dirt-floored room. A shelf held a solitary can without a label. Slocum's belly growled so loudly that he didn't care what was inside. It would be his midday meal.

Going back to his horse for his canteen and gear turned him suddenly uneasy. He looked around but saw no one. Walking to the edge of one of the pits, he peered downward and couldn't tell how deep it was. Before he could pick up a pebble and drop it to see if there was water in the bottom, he heard a small sound, hardly more than a tiny whisper, and knew he was in big trouble.

"Got the drop on you again, Neale," Wilmer said. "You

led me a merry chase, but you ain't so good at hidin' your trail. I'm 'bout the best damn tracker west of the Mississippi."

Slocum dropped some of his gear and turned slowly, his hands away from his sides. Wilmer held an old blackpowder musket on him.

"You still got my smoke wagon? Why don't you go on and toss it back to me."

"This?" Slocum nodded at the six-shooter thrust into his waistband.

"Yep, that's it. Not many men coulda got that away from me. I'll give you that much. Might be I kin ask fer a few extra dollars with you bein' such a slippery gent."

Slocum began edging away from the lip of the pit.

"Now don't go anywhere on me," Wilmer said sharply. "If you want to throw down on me, give 'er a try. You won't git halfway to yer six-shooter."

"You've got me," Slocum said. "But I'm not Neale."

"Now you quit sayin' that. Of course you are. I didn't fall off the turnip wagon this morning. You pull my gun out of your belt real slowlike, but don't go throwin' it onto the ground like before. That's a precise killin' weapon, it is."

Slocum laid his saddlebags down and put Wilmer's pistol on top of them near the edge of the pit. As he straightened, he slid his foot into a strap on the saddlebags and then put his hands up high in the air. Wilmer's gaze followed the hands and ignored the feet.

"I've done what you asked," Slocum said. "What now?"

"Why, I take you on back to Las Vegas and collect the reward. But I got to hogtie you, you bein' so slippery and all."

The bounty hunter moved forward, eyes fixed on Slocum. Slocum jerked his hand about as he held it above his head to keep Wilmer's attention diverted. When Wilmer knelt to pick up his six-shooter, Slocum kicked hard. His toe caught in the leather strap and yanked the saddlebags out from under the six-shooter, sending it skittering toward the pit.

Wilmer yelped and instinctively grabbed for his six-gun. When his attention strayed, Slocum acted. A quick step forward and a hard kick sent the bounty hunter flailing to land at the edge of the pit. As Wilmer grabbed for his gun, Slocum kicked him again. Man and six-gun tumbled into the pit.

A loud splash echoed up.

"That settles the question of whether there's water in the pit."

Slocum picked up his saddlebags and backed from the pit before Wilmer started shooting at anything recklessly poking over the rim of the pit—like Slocum's head.

"You cain't leave me down here!" came the bounty hunter's angry shout.

"Why not?" Slocum said to himself. He returned to the shack, grabbed the can of unknown contents, tucked it into his saddlebags, and then rode away intent on putting as much distance between him and Wilmer as possible. He never wanted to see the bounty hunter again, but he doubted he would be that lucky.

3

It was so peaceful that it made Slocum ache. He had spent the past four days covering his trail, looking over his shoulder, doubling back and riding in wide arcs, all to throw Wilmer off his tracks. Whether the bounty hunter had ever escaped the rocky shaft where Slocum had dumped him hardly mattered, but if he had, Slocum was certain he would be coming fast with blood in his eye.

But Taos stretched quiet and peaceful, the kind of town where nothing violent ever happened. Slocum rode slowly to the plaza, knowing this was an illusion. The first American territorial governor had been brutally killed here during an Indian uprising. This was a terminus for the Bent brothers' vast trading empire and hard battles had been fought here in years past. He could almost smell the blood that had been spilled. Almost. The entire town was taking a siesta right now and it was deceptively peaceful.

Slocum dismounted and went into a cantina just off the plaza. The cool, dim interior of the adobe building wrapped itself around him as the scent of spilled beer rose to make Slocum's nostrils flare. He searched his pockets, wondering if money had mysteriously appeared since he had left Las Vegas. It hadn't. That didn't stop Slocum from going to the bar and leaning his elbows on it. His reflection in the highly polished mirror hanging behind the bar told him he needed more than a drink. He appeared gaunt. The single can of tomatoes taken from the miner's shack hadn't lasted very long, and taking time to hunt would have given Wilmer the chance of overtaking him—a gunshot would have given Slocum's location away to the wary, clever bounty hunter.

"Here," the barkeep said, sliding a tin cup down the bar. Water sloshed onto the stained wood as Slocum reached out to stop the cup. "Unless you're different, that's all you're getting."

"Different?"

"You got money to pay for a drink?" The barkeep eyed Slocum, then laughed ruefully. "Hell, no, I've seen that look too many times lately. And the boss'd have my scalp if I started giving away free drinks."

Slocum downed the water. It was cool and tasted as sweet as any he'd ever drunk. He wiped his lips.

"Much obliged. Don't reckon there's—"

"Any jobs here? None, at least none I've heard about," the barkeep said. He perched on the corner of the bar, his legs swinging idly back and forth like scissors. "Not even guards at the bank." The barkeep gave Slocum the once-over, but his eyes kept dancing back to the pistol at his hip.

"Where's the marshal's office?"

"He's not hiring deputies either."

"You're mighty accommodating," Slocum said.

"Come back when you got money. There's a real fine bottle of pop-skull from Kentucky you might like."

Slocum stepped out into the hot afternoon sun and looked around the plaza. A few citizens moved about now on errands of unknown motivation. Why try to do business when you could be sleeping through the hottest part of the day? Slocum made his way around the plaza hunting for the marshal's office. His heart beat a little faster as he went inside. He wanted to avoid the law whenever he could, but this side trip was necessary if he didn't want to spend his stay in Taos looking over his shoulder for more than a bounty hunter.

The deputy slept with his feet up on the desk. Slocum walked on cat's feet to keep from waking him as he went to a wall festooned with wanted posters. Working through the tattered array failed to reveal any warrant out for a man named Neale. Slocum scanned the wanted posters a second time looking for his own likeness, under any name.

"Wha—?"

Slocum whirled, hand moving to the butt of his six-shooter as the deputy's feet fell from the desktop.

"What you doin', mister?"

"I was looking for the marshal. Is he in?"

"Naw, he's out ridin' circuit. Servin' process and makin' a few extra dollars," the deputy said. "Lucky son of a bitch gets extra money. All he pays me is twenty dollars a month."

The deputy rubbed his eyes and peered more closely at Slocum.

"I know you, mister?"

"Can't say we've met," Slocum said cautiously. There might be a special pile of wanted posters carrying either his likeness or that of the mysterious Neale.

The deputy shook himself and leaned back, studying Slocum more closely.

"Reckon not."

"Are these all the posters you have?" Slocum tapped the wall behind him with his knuckles.

"Yep, all of 'em. We get new ones from time to time. The marshal over in Las Vegas sends 'em along, when he thinks about it. Hasn't sent any in a while. Too hot to ride maybe. Or too lazy. Marshal Hanks ain't what you'd call diligent."

"Is that the Las Vegas marshal?"

"Marshal Hanks? Yeah, that's him. Leroy Hanks. Marshal here's named Rodriguez. Not a bad fellow, but he spends more time workin' for the judge than he does tendin' business here in town. Leaves that to me."

"That's got to mean he thinks a lot of your ability," Slocum said to placate the deputy.

"Never thought of it that way. Always figured he was lettin' me haul away the dead animals out of the streets and handle the drunks so he wouldn't have to do it."

"Taos seems to be mighty calm," Slocum said. "A tribute to the law here, I'd say."

"Never thought about it that way. Yeah, you're right!" With that, the deputy hiked his boots back to the desktop and tipped his hat back down over his eyes. In seconds a steady snoring told exactly how calm it was in town.

Slocum cast one last look at the wall covered with old wanted posters, and heaved a sigh of relief. He might have a bounty hunter and Marshal Hanks after him for no reason, but their mistake hadn't reached Taos yet. The heat wrapped him like cotton wool, but he felt good for the first time since riding into Las Vegas. He liked Taos and might stay a while, if he could find a job. Things were as hard here as over in Las Vegas, at least when it came to gainful employment.

Heading for the public watering trough in the plaza to dunk his head and cool off, he stopped when he heard an argument getting more heated by the second. Normally he wouldn't have interfered, but the woman standing just inside the doorway of the general store presented a mighty fine side to him. She had a wasp waist and was curvy in all the right places otherwise. When she turned, Slocum caught her profile. A fine, straight, patrician nose, thin lips, and firm chin were momentarily obscured by a strand of mahogany-colored hair that escaped from under her broad-brimmed hat. With a nervous gesture she brushed the hair away as she kept up a rapid and increasingly loud argument. She stamped her foot and turned back so her face was hidden. A soft swish of her cambric dress or the crinkle of her starched white blouse could not drown out a deeper masculine reply.

"That's not right. You can't mean it," she said. Her voice echoed shrilly, but Slocum thought it was from her agitation. He shielded his eyes from the sun and saw she had stepped into the general store.

A torrent of Spanish seemed to confuse the woman. Slocum licked his dried lips, then decided a dousing in the water trough could wait a few minutes.

"Ma'am," he said, entering the store, touching the brim of his hat. "Is something wrong?"

"This, this . . . gentleman is trying to rob me! He wants me to pay five times what these supplies are worth. When I complained, he began yammering away in Spanish."

"And you don't understand Spanish," Slocum guessed. He saw by the frown on her lovely face that she did not. What she did understand, though, was the outdoors. She was no hothouse flower, pale and fluttery. She had a deep tan that contrasted just enough with her reddish-brown hair to look healthy and just a tad exotic because of her violet eyes.

"There are not many who speak that language where I hail from," she said almost apologetically.

"*Señor*," began the proprietor of the general store. "*La mujer está loca. Ella—*"

Slocum held up his hand to shut off the flood of recrimination.

"Let me speak with her a moment," Slocum said. The clerk shrugged expressively as if saying they both knew she was crazy but Slocum could do as he wished, devil take the hindmost.

Slocum took the woman's arm and guided her just outside the store.

"What are you in the market for?"

"I beg your pardon!"

"What do you want to buy from that unhung road agent?"

"Oh," she said contritely. "I thought you meant—never mind. I need supplies to go into the mountains for at least two weeks. A month would be better."

"You have any gear or are you buying it all?"

"Why, I have my personal belongings. Clothing, other items, but nothing I need to, well, live."

"You don't want to live off the land? You aren't going to hunt?"

"I wouldn't know how," she said. "It's frowned upon when people shoot anything in Chicago."

Slocum had figured she was a city girl. But she didn't have the pallor he usually associated with those who stayed indoors all the time. When she reached out to lay her hand on his arm, he saw calluses. She was used to hard work, in spite of her citified, highfalutin clothing with its pearl buttons and precisely stitched seams.

"First time out West?" Slocum asked.

"Well, yes, it is," she admitted. "I have work to do."

"What sort?" She stiffened and put a little distance between them. Her hand slipped from his arm, indicating her reluctance to talk of her business with a total stranger. "Not that it matters. You need the supplies, and he's trying to cheat you? Is that it in a nutshell?"

She nodded and smiled at him almost shyly.

Slocum went into the store and pawed through the stack of supplies the woman intended buying. He saw a few luxuries like tooth powder and soap, but mostly she had chosen well for a month-long stay in the mountains. Not too much, but enough. Beautiful and practical, he decided.

Slocum began his dickering in English, but quickly changed to Spanish when the proprietor did so. They changed in and out of both languages, with hand gestures and stomping around on the dirt floor until tiny clouds hung about. Slocum was aware of the woman watching from just outside the door, her hand at her mouth as if she feared there would be gunplay.

Finally Slocum turned and asked, "How much are you willing to pay for all this? He's asking eighteen dollars, but that's too much." He stared hard at her, hoping she would take the cue. She was quick as well as pretty.

"Oh, no, that's far too much," she said, looking irritated. Pretty, smart, and a talented actress when called for.

"*Lo siento,*" Slocum said, pushing at the stack of supplies with his foot.

"*No, no, un momento, señor, por favor!*"

Another few minutes had the proprietor slumping and bemoaning the fate of his business, his starving children, and the entire town of Taos at such thievery.

"Fourteen dollars," Slocum said. "That's a good price and not likely to be improved on."

"Done!" She came over, worked in a small clutch purse, and handed over the fourteen dollars in gold and silver coins. The store owner held out his hands as she counted the proper amount.

"I'll give you a hand with these," Slocum said, moving the stacks of goods outside. He left everything in the shade but away from the door.

"Thank you, sir. You've been a big help," she said, gracing him with a bright smile.

"I could have gotten him down at least another six bits if I'd known you were paying in specie. I thought you were going to pay in greenbacks."

"I understand the difference. Paper money's not worth a great deal, is it?"

"A ten-percent discount is customary for hard metal, unless the scrip is written on a local bank. You can usually get a discount for coin since a store like this deals with a lot of travelers who won't take anything else."

"You are quite knowledgeable, as well as helpful."

She paused, at a loss for words. Slocum helped her out by introducing himself.

"I am so rude," she said, blushing a mite. "My name's

Claudia Peterson." She thrust out her hand as if she expected him to shake it as he would a man's hand. Slocum obliged.

"Miss Peterson, can I load your supplies into a wagon?" Slocum looked around, but saw nothing that looked like a buggy.

"I have a buckboard out back," she said. "Let me bring it around."

"You stay out of the sun," Slocum said. He had nothing better to do than spend a few more minutes with this lovely woman. Truth to tell, he was curious as to why she traveled alone, needed a month's worth of supplies, and intended to drive off into the Sangre de Cristo Mountains.

He found the buckboard and checked it. The wagon had seen better days but looked sturdy enough. How well it would fare off the twin-rutted roads around Taos was something else. He hopped into the driver's seat, took the reins, and got the team pulling. They were old horses, both mares, and weren't about to be hurried. Again, Slocum reflected on Claudia's common sense. This team might not have the strength of younger horses, but they weren't likely to be wild and uncontrollable either.

He halted the team in a spot where it wouldn't take much effort to load the supplies. Claudia knelt by one pile, carefully going through and checking off everything from a list.

"You're mighty well organized," Slocum said, jumping down. "Any particular way you want this loaded?"

"You know best," she said. Claudia started to say something more, but hesitated. Slocum quickly loaded her supplies. By then she had worked up her courage.

"Here, Mr. Slocum," she said, handing over a silver cartwheel. "I appreciate your intervention on my part. That man would have rooked me out of far more than this."

Slocum looked at the shining silver dollar and almost

reached for it. His upbringing prevented him from taking money for being polite to a woman.

"No thanks, Miss Peterson. Your presence is payment enough."

"Ah, the Southern gentleman. Please. I insist." She grabbed his hand and pressed it on him. Visions of beer and a decent meal flashed through Slocum's head. He needed supplies himself, mostly ammunition, if he wanted to ride on. This wasn't enough for all that, but it was a start.

"Thank you," he said, tucking the large coin into his vest pocket. "Are you going to hit the trail tomorrow?"

"I'd hoped to, get a start now," Claudia said. "I've wasted so much time."

"Mind if I ask what you're looking for out in the mountains? There are some dangers there you aren't likely to find in a town like Chicago."

She laughed and said, "Have you ever been to Chicago, Mr. Slocum?" He had to admit that he had not. "There are dangerous animals of all kinds there, and I deal with them well."

"Be careful," Slocum said. "But you never answered what you were hunting for out there."

"What makes you think I'm hunting for something?" she said sharply.

"You don't look like a miner or homesteader," Slocum said. "That cuts down on most reasons you'd go into rugged hills like those." He jerked his thumb over his shoulder in the direction of the towering peaks.

"I . . . I am an artist. I am here to paint landscapes. When I pick up my easel and canvases—and my paint box, of course—I'll be off."

Her hesitation made Slocum think she waited for him to volunteer to accompany her. It wouldn't be proper for a re-fined lady like Claudia Peterson appeared to be to come out and ask, but Slocum thought wandering around meadows and watching her paint pretty pictures wasn't something he wanted to do. As lovely as she was, Claudia was all business. If there had been a hint that she might expect more from a guide, Slocum might have been interested.

"Have a safe trip," Slocum said, touching the brim of his hat. Claudia looked crestfallen, but covered it well with a wan smile.

"Thank you, Mr. Slocum." He helped her into the driver's box. She took the reins and expertly got the buckboard moving smoothly as she circled the plaza and started out of town. Slocum returned to the saloon, the silver dollar burning a hole in his pocket. He stopped dead in his tracks when he saw a familiar man going into the saloon.

Marshal Hanks.

Slocum let him disappear into the dim, quiet cantina, and then fetched his horse from the shady side of the saloon. As he walked his distinctive Appaloosa around front, he heard Hanks's loud voice asking, "You see this varmint any time in the past few days?" A rustle of paper was followed by the barkeep's mumbled, unintelligible reply.

Slocum didn't want to know if the barkeep had identified him as Neale. He swung into the saddle, put his spurs to the horse's flanks, and overtook Claudia within a quarter mile. She was on the outskirts of Taos, heading into rugged country.

From her big smile when he asked if he could guide her for a spell, he knew she was glad to have his company. He just hoped she would be willing to lie for him if Marshal Hanks came hunting him down.

4

Slocum tried not to be obvious every time he glanced over his shoulder at the back trail for any sign of pursuit, but Claudia noticed.

"What's wrong, Mr. Slocum?" She snapped the reins of the team expertly and got the horses pulling up a steep incline to the top of a hill. "You seem nervous. Is there trouble brewing?"

"No, no trouble for you," he said. "I have some men on my trail who have mistaken me for someone else."

"How unfortunate," she said. "This man they have mistaken you for? He's an outlaw?"

Slocum hesitated before answering. He had no idea why the marshal or Wilmer wanted Neale, but it had to be for something considerably illegal to warrant a hundred-dollar reward. From what he had seen of the nearsighted station agent in Las Vegas yammering at the marshal after a closer look at Slocum's face, that was most likely the source of the misidentification.

"It'd sound like I was lying if I said I haven't got a clue why they want this owlhoot, but it's the truth."

"Then I believe you," she said almost primly. "You are an honest man."

"You don't know that," Slocum said.

"I am considered a good judge of human nature," Claudia said. She smiled. "I'm not wrong about you, am I?"

"Depends on what you think of me," he said. A blush came to her cheeks and she looked away abruptly to hide it. "Why not rest the team a few minutes?" he suggested. "They've had a hard pull this far."

"What will you do? Double back to see if anyone is actually on our trail?"

"*My* trail," he corrected. "This isn't your fight."

"I choose to make it so," she said, sounding like that prim schoolmarm again. But the blush in her cheeks lingered, giving her something of an innocent look.

"I won't be long," Slocum said. And he wasn't. He rode in a sweeping arc that took him away from the ruts that passed for a road and over to a spot where he got a better look at the road stretching a mile back toward Taos. No one came after him, not that he could see, but he had to remind himself that Wilmer was an expert at sneaking up on him. Slocum doubted the man was overly intelligent, but he had mountain man skills that made him dangerous—doubly so if Slocum ever underestimated him. This was why Slocum doubted Wilmer was still at the bottom of the mine shaft.

Slocum sat astride his Appaloosa, watching the road and thinking hard. He could return to Taos and slip past Marshal Hanks and be on his way to Santa Fe before Claudia even realized he was gone. That was the smart thing to do. In spite of her determination, his trouble with Hanks and Wilmer wasn't her business and would only bring her woe. Still, Slocum reflected, she was alone in a land she knew nothing about and deserved a decent guide.

He swung his horse around and returned to the hilltop where Claudia waited patiently.

"Well?" she asked. "Do the hordes of hell nip at our heels?"

"Not a whiff of brimstone," he assured her. He studied

her face for a moment, and wondered if he would regret continuing to guide Claudia through the mountains. Somehow, seeing the expression on her face, he doubted it.

"I would like to paint at a spot nearby. Is there something scenic?"

Slocum shrugged. He had no idea what she meant. The mountains were something to cross, to fight against, to keep from killing him. Rivers provided drinking water.

"A canyon would be nice. Is there one I might study and possibly paint?"

"The Rio Grande cuts through the land ahead. I was going around the gorge since there's no way to go down and then back up the far side with a buckboard. Or even on horseback. The sides of the gorge are mighty steep."

"That sounds perfect," she said enthusiastically. "How far is it?"

Slocum got his bearings, then pointed. "About an hour's ride in that direction."

" 'Scout 'em and flout 'em,' " she said. Seeing Slocum's quizzical look, Claudia explained. "Shakespeare. You have read the immortal Bard, haven't you, Mr. Slocum?"

"Can't say that I have."

"You do read?"

"When I have to," Slocum said, enjoying how she became flustered at his seeming illiteracy as they rode along.

"An education is the most important thing a man can possess," she said.

"Depends on your need." Slocum tapped his Colt Navy. "Given the right—or wrong—situation, I'd rather have this with six rounds loaded into the cylinder than a book of sonnets."

She saw that he was joshing her. "Sonnets, Mr. Slocum? You know that Shakespeare wrote sonnets?"

"I must have picked that up when I was down South. In Shakespeare, New Mexico."

"There's such a place?"

"Surely is," he said, "but it's not the sort of place where you'd be too comfortable. Last time I was through, they hung a fellow from the rafters, then hid and waited for the stagecoach to come through. The passengers got out to stretch their legs and found the hanged man. The citizens of the town got a powerful lot of amusement out of their reactions."

"How awful," Claudia said, shivering a little. Slocum couldn't help noticing the way her blouse bobbed and bounced about when she moved like that. The jostling of the wagon only added to her allure.

"Entertainment's hard to come by in places like that," Slocum said.

Claudia didn't answer. They made their way down to a dry river bottom, then up to a level plain that seemed to stretch for twenty miles.

"This is where you said there would be scenic terrain?" She looked at him as if he were joking with her again.

"Keep driving, but not too fast. You don't want to go over the edge of the canyon."

"Canyon? What canyon? I hear a river but—oh!" Claudia pulled back hard on the reins, secured them, and stood, staring at the Rio Grande and the gorge it had slashed in the level plains. "That *is* scenic. You know exactly what I wanted, Mr. Slocum."

"What's that?" he asked. Again, he flustered her as she blushed and struggled to find the proper words.

"Why, this, of course. The scenery is superb, unlike anything I have ever seen."

"There's a bigger hole in the ground over in Arizona," he said, "but this one's closer." Slocum studied the colorful rock layers in the far canyon wall all the way down to the Rio Grande rushing along furiously at the bottom of a two-hundred-foot deep gash. The drought might have dried up the Rio Grande farther south, but not here. Taos could get all the water it needed, but the stretch of thirsty desert farther south sucked up most all of the liquid. But here, there was no drought. Slocum thumped his canteen and noted it was almost empty.

"This will do just fine. Where should I set up the easel to paint?"

"Should we go to the bottom or do you want to stay up here on the rim?"

"We can go to the river?" Claudia looked skeptical.

"It'd take another couple days of hard travel either north or south to get away from this gorge and to a spot where we could work our way down. The sides are nowhere near as steep in other places."

"Let's do both," she said. "I'll paint here for a day or two; then we can go down and see what vista I can achieve there."

"We're exposed to the elements out here. We should find a place where there's more shelter."

"Where might that be? The nearest trees are miles off. All I see are scrubby bushes."

"There must be rocks around here where we could camp. I'll go take a look."

"Scout and flout," she called as he rode off to the north. He had to laugh. He hadn't lied when he said he wasn't much of a Shakespeare reader, but he had heard of the man. There just never seemed much purpose in reading anything by a Brit dead more than two hundred years. Better to keep an eye out for wanted posters with his name on them—or Neale's. Slocum found a likely campsite after a half hour of hunting. A ring of rocks more than head high provided a decent windbreak, there was adequate firewood nearby, and more important to Slocum, it was out of sight of the road running along the gorge.

He tethered his horse and let it graze on a patch of blue grama, climbed to the top of the tallest boulder, and used his field glasses to scan the entire region, starting at the road and working in a full circle. His heart jumped when he saw a dust cloud to the north, cutting off any retreat in that direction.

Watching for several minutes set his heart racing even more. Somehow, Marshal Hanks had swung around and gotten between Slocum and the way leading west across the Rio Grande. Slocum lowered his binoculars and wondered if he ought to have it out with the lawman. There wasn't any reasoning with him, Slocum realized, since the lawman had left his bailiwick and pursued him this far. A marshal's authority didn't extend beyond the city limits unless he was a federal marshal. From the brief glimpse Slocum had had of Leroy Hanks's badge, the man wasn't authorized to make arrests out here.

"What's Neale done to make him such a desperado?" Slocum wondered aloud. There was no answer unless he had it out with the lawman, and that meant one of them wouldn't ride away. Slocum didn't see any reason for that to happen. All he wanted was to be left alone.

Slocum then saw that Hanks was riding straight for Claudia Peterson. Slocum chewed his lower lip, wondering what she would do when the lawman began questioning her. It was lucky that Slocum had taken off to scout a camp for them. Otherwise, he would have been caught with her. But he found himself faced with a serious dilemma. He could ride out, heading north in the direction Hanks had come from, make it across the Rio Grande, and be lost in the depths of the mountains to the north, or he could wait. Going to confront the marshal as he spoke with Claudia would do no good, other than to put the woman's life in jeopardy.

Run or wait?

Slocum waited. He grabbed his field glasses and followed the marshal's rapid progress directly to where Claudia painted. Slocum wished he could soar like a hawk and peer down to see what was happening. He played out what the conversation might be like repeatedly, to no avail. There was nothing he could do to change the outcome. The marshal might come after him after being put on his trail by the woman.

He might even believe her lies if she said she had no idea where Slocum was. That hardly seemed likely since Slocum doubted she was much at lying. The way she blushed would give her away.

Slocum sat on the rock to limit his silhouette against the sky, braced his elbows on his lifted knees, and studied the terrain in the direction where Hanks would come from. For an hour he sat and waited until a dust cloud rose. He straightened, then stood, trying to make out the rider in the middle of the cloud. When it got close enough, Slocum saw Claudia Peterson snapping the reins on her team and coming toward him.

He tried to peer through the dust to see if Hanks followed, but he couldn't. Slocum waved, and Claudia veered from her course and came toward the rocks he had chosen for their camp.

"There was a marshal!" she called by way of greeting. "He asked if I had seen a solitary rider and described you, John. I was so scared!"

"What did you tell him?"

"I . . . I lied!" She made it sound like a major accomplishment to be proud of. "I told him I hadn't seen anyone answering to your description. He must have believed me because he thanked me and kept riding south."

Slocum turned his field glasses in that direction. The dust had blown away giving a better view. He saw nothing to show that Marshal Hanks was within ten miles.

"Why did you lie?" Slocum asked.

"I . . . he was a disagreeable man, that's why. And you had told me there might be people asking after you because of that confusion. He didn't call you Slocum. He said Neale every time."

"Thanks," Slocum said. He slid off the rock and landed

on his feet, brushed off the dirt, and then began digging a firepit in the middle of a sandy spit. A few rocks provided a lining for it, and he began gathering firewood.

"You aren't going to ask anything more about him?" Claudia stared wide-eyed at him, her violet eyes innocent.

"You said about all that I needed to hear," Slocum replied. "It's surprising that he left Las Vegas to hunt for this Neale so far afield. Did the marshal happen to mention what Neale is wanted for?"

Claudia shook her head.

"I'll rustle up a rabbit, or we could fix something out of your supplies."

"That'll be fine," she said distantly. Claudia moved about as if in a daze. He heard her mutter to herself, "I lied to a lawman. I lied!"

He rummaged through the supplies and found some bacon. He also saw the painting she had worked on back at the lip of the gorge.

"Not bad work," he said. "It looks like the outline of the rim."

"It's only a sketch," she said. "I can finish it later. Now, I want as many sketches as I can do. What are you doing?"

Slocum had pushed aside the blank canvases and found a completed picture of mountains dotted with mines and a valley like the ones he had ridden through to reach Taos.

"This is mighty fine. Almost like a photograph."

"Put it back. You aren't to even look at that one!"

"Sorry," he said, wondering why she had gotten so frantic.

"I overreacted. It . . . it's just that I'm not used to anyone looking at my paintings."

"Isn't the idea of a painting for other people to appreciate it?"

"Yes, of course, but not this one."

Slocum took one last look at it before returning it to the pile.

"Looks a lot like the country I traveled getting to Taos."

"You—"

Slocum clamped his hand over her mouth. He heard a small sound, barely detectable, but distinctive. A horse nickered, and it wasn't one of theirs.

"There's a bounty hunter on my trail too. I'm afraid he's found me." Claudia struggled to speak, but Slocum kept his hand over her mouth. "He won't be as pleasant as the marshal. If the bounty hunter asks, you tell him the truth. I rode north, intending to cross the river. Do you understand? Just nod if you do."

Claudia bobbed her head.

"Remember, it's important you tell him the whole truth. Everything I just said." Slocum heard more soft sounds as someone searched the far side of the rocks.

"Are you sure, John?"

"My life depends on it," he said. "I've got to go. Now."

As he turned, she grabbed him and said urgently, "Wait. Wait a moment."

He swung around to find her in his arms. She planted a big kiss on his lips and then pushed away, blushing. Slocum reached out and touched her cheek. It was warm under his fingertips.

"Good-bye," he said softly. Then he jumped onto his horse and walked away slowly, being as quiet as possible. The faint sounds might have been his imagination, but he doubted it. As he put the rocks between him and Claudia, he heard a loud cry of triumph. He recognized Wilmer's voice.

Slocum sped up, trotting off, then letting his horse break into a gallop to put as much distance between him and the bounty hunter as possible. It was getting dark so Slocum took the opportunity to take a creosote bush and drag it behind to cover his tracks. He doubled back once and rode at an angle to the trail he wanted to lead the bounty hunter astray. Then he cut directly for the gorge.

The canyon walls two miles north weren't as steep, but still afforded no way to get down to the river. He kept riding, taking care to erase his path from time to time before he found the proper trail to the Rio Grande.

Imagining Wilmer thundering along behind him, chortling as he found every feeble attempt to hide the trail, Slocum began work on a real diversion. He started across a rocky patch, left a single hoofprint on the far side, and then backed over another rocky stretch before heading due east. If Lady Luck so decreed, Wilmer would plunge downward to the river, hunting for Slocum where he had not gone. It might be days before the bounty hunter realized his mistake—or never.

Slocum was as expert as any man when it came to tracking and misleading trackers.

His only regret as he headed east into the mountains was leaving Claudia Peterson behind.

5

If he had properly decoyed Wilmer, it would take the bounty hunter more than a few days to get to the bottom of the deep gorge, hunt for more tracks, then return to the rim and search anew for Slocum's actual trail. With a little weather and a lot of luck, Slocum's trail would be obliterated and he would be safely on his way through the Sangre de Cristo Mountains, staying well north of Las Vegas once he got back out on the eastern plains. Turning north and entering Colorado through Raton Pass was his best bet for getting away from both the law and bounty hunters running rampant in New Mexico.

His only regret was leaving Claudia Peterson on her own. She had been determined to do her scenic painting alone, so his departure didn't affect her plans that much, but this was dangerous wilderness compared to downtown Chicago, no matter what she said. And she was a mighty pretty filly. He wouldn't have minded spending some time getting to know her.

His hand drifted up and rubbed his dried lips as he remembered her kiss. It had been unexpected, probably for both of them. Claudia didn't look like the sort to pass out her affections easily. Slocum smiled a little, wondering what was pushing her so hard. He had known an artist or two in his day, and he suspected most of them had been nibbling at loco weed, but Claudia didn't seem driven like they were by passion. She was more controlled, reserved, even inhibited to the point of not talking about her artwork. That was entirely different from all the others Slocum had known. Once they were asked about their work, they never shut up.

From what Slocum had seen of her sketch and the completed picture amid the blank canvases, she was a top-notch artist and ought to have been eager to find someone interested and appreciative. Slocum rubbed his lips again, then reached for his canteen. The cold metal rim and wetness dribbling into his mouth were nothing like Claudia's kiss.

He looked into the mountains to find a pass that would get him out and onto the plains north of Las Vegas. Thinking of her wasn't going to do his peace of mind any good. Mostly he regretted things that had never happened rather than ones that had—and his life had been filled with intense violence—but turning around and rejoining her on her artistic cavalcade wouldn't do either of them any good.

Wilmer was too single-minded in his attempts to capture Neale, and judging from the way Marshal Hanks had left his own jurisdiction, he might be as eager to put a notch on his six-shooter handle as Wilmer.

"What did Neale do and why are they so anxious to catch him?" Slocum wondered aloud. It did no good pondering this mysterious crime. He had enough of his own under his belt to worry about.

He reached the foothills and slipped easily back onto higher ground, finding the pass he had taken earlier to reach Taos. This time he was heading back in the direction of Las Vegas, but he remembered branching canyons that went to the northeast that he was sure would deliver him to the exact spot he wanted. And if they didn't, he was still going northerly and away from both the bounty hunter and the marshal.

As he rode, he reflected on how much this country looked like the picture Claudia had drawn. She must have come through these canyons with their played-out mines and steep sides before he had found her in Taos arguing with the general store owner. But Slocum frowned as this thought flitted across his mind. Had she done only one painting? And where had she come from that she was out of supplies? She might have come from Las Vegas and more or less followed the trail Slocum had, though it had been a rough one. There were myriad ways through these mountains, and she must have taken a different path since he hadn't seen any fresh ruts left by a buckboard.

He rode deeper into the hills and looked around more, head swiveling from one side to the other in constant surveillance of his surroundings. The painting Claudia had done looked similar to these hills, but not exactly. He hadn't gotten that good a look at her work, being distracted by other things including the artist herself, but the placement of the mines was all wrong. Too many on one side of the canyon and too few on the other to match her painting. Slocum shrugged it off. There was no reason she couldn't have taken artistic license to improve the composition by adding or subtracting mines and other features. Art wasn't the same as a photograph.

Slocum rested a spell at the base of a steep incline, then started his Appaloosa up it. The horse had a hard time making progress in the loose gravel, but eventually reached the summit to give Slocum a good look ahead. The green valley curved away, lush and inviting. A stream ran down the middle and wooded spots all around promised game. He was tired of rabbit and might bag a deer. Venison would go down mighty good after the gamy, tough rabbit meat he had been living on because it was easy to get.

His horse neighed and tossed its head, anxious to get

into the meadowlands and graze on the graze. Slocum wasn't inclined to hold the Appaloosa back.

The shot echoing through the valley sounded far off, distant, of no importance to Slocum. Then his horse took a stumbling step. The second attempt to move a leg caused the Appaloosa to sag and begin to fall. Slocum kicked free of the stirrups and got his leg from under the falling horse before it pinned him to the ground. He rolled on the rocky ground and then reversed course and fetched up hard against his horse. It wasn't breathing. A few seconds of examination revealed the bullet hole just above its front legs. The slug had gone straight through the valiant horse's heart, killing it instantly.

Slocum peered up from the horse's carcass as he tried to find the sniper. The echo from the rifle had died down, leaving only an eerie silence that told Slocum more than anything else, the sniper was still out there, and the rampant wildlife in the valley was quiet until the danger vanished.

Fumbling, Slocum worked to get his rifle from its sheath. The horse had fallen on that side, pinning the rifle between dead flesh and rock. As Slocum worked, a dust cloud puffed up inches from his face. The rifle report came a fraction of a second later. He jerked hard and got his Winchester free. Dropping behind the bulwark provided by the horse's body, Slocum settled himself and got his wits back about him. Everything had happened so fast, he wasn't sure what was going on. The second shot convinced him the man lying in ambush had wanted to kill him and not his horse.

An accidental round would never have been followed by a second.

Slocum chanced a quick peek around the horse. A patch of woods a hundred yards away had to provide the concealment for the sniper. Nothing closer would hide a rifle, much less the man bringing it to his shoulder to murder Slocum.

The lack of cover between the horse and the woods worked against Slocum. He couldn't edge closer so his first shot would be the last needed. If anything, the sniper had him in a nasty position. As long as he remained hidden behind his dead horse, he was safe. Retreating up the hill, going ahead into the valley, or staging a frontal assault on the woods would all result in one thing—his death. The sharpshooter had proven his skill with such a long shot being off by only inches. Slocum could make such a shot in return, but he had no visible target.

Since it was out of the question for him to reach safety in three directions, Slocum rolled onto his back, supported his head against his saddle, and looked to the left of the trail he had been following into the valley. The horse provided some protection if he crawled, but the rocky ground would make that retreat a pure hell.

Slocum started, the sharp stones cutting at his belly and chest, nicking his knees and doing some small damage to his hands as he scuttled along. Three more shots followed him, but they went high. When he made it over a bulge in the hill, he was safe from any more gunfire, but he didn't rest. He sprinted for the summit of the hill and got over it, moving fast to circle around and approach the sniper from his flank.

He slowed as he came upon a few spindly trees, then drifted from behind one trunk to the next until he found a spot about where the sniper must have shot from. Two bright spent brass cartridges on the ground caught Slocum's attention. Stretching his imagination, he saw a man stretched prone, waiting, aiming, firing. But that was his imagination. Slocum looked around carefully and didn't see anyone who might have ambushed him. He knelt and then walked in a crouch to where the ambusher had been, found crushed pine needles leading in the direction of the valley.

Slocum raced in that direction, throwing caution to the

winds. The sniper wouldn't be expecting him right away. The quicker he fought back, the more likely he was to take the backshooting son of a bitch by surprise.

He burst out of the forest into a clearing in time to see a rider fifty yards away riding off.

Slocum lifted his rifle, controlled his breathing, let out a gusty sigh, squeezed, and fired. He knew as his finger came back that it was a true shot. Slocum looked up over the barrel and saw the distant owlhoot throw his hands into the air and tumble from horseback. Slocum cursed when the horse reared and then bolted into the distant woods.

He slogged across the clearing and got to the man's side. Slocum took grim satisfaction in his shot. He had shattered the man's spine. Marksmanship aside, he wished he had left the ambusher alive so he could find out why he had been the man's target. Slocum rolled the man over and stared at him, trying to remember if he had ever seen him before. He was a complete stranger.

Rummaging through his pockets turned out four wadded-up greenbacks and a twenty-dollar gold piece. Slocum grunted as he moved them to his own pocket. He was suddenly rich because this corpse had tried to murder him. He continued digging, but found nothing, not even a compass or a map to show how the man had arrived at this particular valley hidden away in the eastern stretch of the Sangre de Cristo Mountains.

Slocum stood and listened hard for the runaway horse's hoofbeats. He heard nothing. Once more all was still, the normal, natural sounds muted. He reached down, plucked the dead man's six-shooter from his holster, and tucked it into his belt. Something told Slocum this gent hadn't ridden alone.

He set off after the frightened horse, needing it if he wasn't going to spend the next week walking. Tracking the horse for a few hundred yards was easy. The frightened animal had left heavy prints in the soft ground throughout the forested area, but when Slocum reached the other side of the woods, it turned rockier. He wiped sweat from his forehead and got to work, hunting for scratches on the rocks and bent or broken twigs on the low-growing bushes.

His hard work paid off less than an hour later when he spotted the horse nervously cropping at a patch of grass poking up through cracks in a rocky pasture. He looked around, saw no one, and then began approaching the skittish horse a few feet at a time. Slocum took a few breaks in his advance to give the horse time to get used to thinking of him as something other than a threat. Now and again the horse raised its head, looked as if it might race off, only to return to its grazing.

Fifteen minutes after finding the horse, Slocum stood beside it, patting its neck, holding its bridle firmly.

"You're not half the horse that the one shot out from under me was, but you'll do," Slocum said. The gray had been neglected from the look of the bones poking through its side and the constant nervous jerks of its head, but Slocum was good with horses and didn't try to mount right away. He checked the hooves and got a pebble out from under one shoe, then stood and let the horse get used to his smell, his presence.

When he finally climbed into the saddle, the gray accepted his weight without hesitation. Slocum turned its head and rode back to where his Appaloosa had been killed to pick up his gear.

Barely had he reached the green valley and turned upslope when the horse reared, pawed at the air, and tried to run.

"Whoa, whoa there," Slocum said, wondering what had spooked the horse.

Then he saw. Two men popped up from behind rocks and began blazing away with their six-shooters. The range was too much for accurate shooting, but so much flying lead had to hit something. One entered the gray's chest and brought it to its knees. Slocum went down with it, unable to get free as he had before. With one leg pinned between deadweight and the ground, he tried to work free.

The two gunmen started toward him, firing as they came. Slocum's rifle had gone flying and lay out of his reach, but he had both his Colt Navy and the six-gun taken off the dead sniper. He pulled the outlaw's gun from his belt and sat up the best he could, resting his hand on the side of the dead horse. Slocum began firing as accurately as he could, which was accurate enough to wing one of the advancing men. When the six-gun came up empty, Slocum tossed it aside and began using his more accurate Colt. He took off the second man's hat, then flopped flat on his back when both of the owlhoots began firing fast. He heard more than one bullet hit the horse's belly.

Slocum let out a loud cry of pain and waited. He had four rounds left and intended to make them count.

"We got 'im, Dusty."

"You sure? I can't tell," said a skeptical Dusty.

"I'm sure. That's Pack's horse. I recognized it right off."

"Yeah, it's Pack's, but that wasn't Pack astride 'er."

"So Pack's dead. No loss. And that one's dead too. Along with the horse."

"We should check the saddlebags," Dusty said.

"Why? Pack never had nuthin' worth stealin'." He laughed harshly. "He was always too busy tryin' to rob us to make a dollar fer himself."

The two continued to argue while Slocum waited impatiently. He had a pair of rounds for each of them. There wasn't likely any other way to prevent them from future ambushes, and Slocum was up to the chore. His finger remained light on the trigger, keeping away a tenseness that might cause him to miss, for what seemed an eternity.

Finally tiring of the wait, he rose up a bit and looked around. The two road agents were gone. They had decided there wasn't anything worth stealing out of Pack's saddle-bags. Or maybe they were worried Slocum was laying a trap of them and had run like the cowards they were.

It didn't matter to Slocum. He was still trapped under the horse. He checked once more to be sure they were gone, then laid aside his six-gun where he could grab it fast if he needed it, then began digging in the ground to free his leg. More than an hour later, Slocum got to his feet, limped about to get circulation back in his leg, and finally walked easily again.

Unlike the two outlaws, he had no idea what he would find in Pack's saddlebags. After a cursory search, he realized they had known their partner better than he expected. There was nothing in the saddlebags worth taking, much less stealing.

He grabbed his rifle, worked the outlaw's rifle free, and then set off for the slope where his Appaloosa would be gathering flies by now. Footsore and tired by the time he reached the dead horse, Slocum sank to the ground and tried to cool off. He needed to find a pond and soak his feet, but right now he wanted to free his saddlebags and get back onto the trail north.

Slinging his saddlebags over his shoulder, juggling two rifles, and disgusted that he had to leave his saddle behind, Slocum set out again, keeping a sharp lookout for the men who had run off thinking he was dead.

If he spotted them before they saw him, they'd be the ones pushing up daisies.

Alert as he was, Slocum was still startled when he saw Claudia Peterson in her buckboard ahead of him.

6

Slocum dropped his load and stared. He wasn't sure if Claudia looked more surprised at finding him here.

"John!" she called, waving.

He trooped ahead, climbing over some rocks and then dropping down in front of the wagon.

"What are you doing here? Your painting finished over at the Rio Grande?"

"It . . . it was getting crowded there. All the people asking after you, so I decided to come this way and . . . and paint," she finished somewhat lamely. Slocum wondered what she had intended to say. Whatever it was, it would have been more honest. Claudia didn't lie very well, and he ought to warn her against getting into poker games.

"Did the marshal come back?"

"He did," she said. "And that terrible, smelly man in the fringed coat."

"Buckskin?"

"Yes, that's what it's called. Wilmer was his name. He was fit to be tied he was so mad. You must have done something terrible to him." Claudia looked innocent, but the way her eyes danced told him she was amused that he had somehow turned the tables on the bounty hunter.

"I out-tracked him," Slocum said.

"If walking is the way you did it, you'll continue doing so." She licked her lips and thought hard before asking, "Would you like a ride?"

"My horse got shot out from under me," Slocum said.

"What? Wilmer? Did he do it? Why, he's worse than I ever thought, shooting a poor horse!"

"Wasn't Wilmer," Slocum said. "Not sure who it was. Likely outlaws out to carve a niche for themselves."

"Here? There's nothing to steal here."

Slocum looked at her closely. Her voice almost broke, and it wasn't with fear. It was something else that he couldn't identify.

"I'll fetch my saddle and the rest of my gear. Surely did not like the idea of leaving it out here, but there's only so much I can carry." Slocum dropped his saddlebags and rifles into the bed of Claudia's buckboard. He saw her intent gaze fixed on the second rifle. "I took it off the outlaw who shot my horse," he said.

"Oh."

Slocum climbed into the box and took the reins from her. She resisted for a moment, then relinquished them to him. Slocum turned the buckboard around and returned to his dead Appaloosa. It took only a few minutes to worry the saddle free from the horse and get it and the bridle tossed into the rear of the wagon.

"Much obliged to you giving me a ride," he said. "My feet were mighty sore, and I hadn't been walking but a few minutes."

"I'm glad for the company," she said, and again Slocum heard an undercurrent that didn't jibe with her words. She *was* glad to see him, but also wished she had never come across him. Claudia Peterson was turning into a mystery that Slocum increasingly wanted to solve.

"Have you been here before?" he asked. "In this part of the mountains?"

"Why do you ask?"

"The painting in the back of the wagon looks like this terrain," he said.

"How?" Her question came sharp and demanding.

"The mines, the shape and color of the mountains, other details," he answered. "It was a compliment. I think you did a good job of capturing what the territory looks like," Slocum said.

"Did you see anywhere that matched the picture?"

"Not exactly," Slocum said. "What's the matter? Don't you remember where you painted it?"

"No," she said, heaving a sigh of relief as if he had given her an escape route. "I wandered around and got lost. I'm not too good at navigating, I fear. C-could you help me find the spot again?"

Slocum considered Wilmer on his trail, and Marshal Hanks still poking around hunting for him. There were dozens of places he could have gone after leaving the Rio Grande gorge, and the chances of them coming this way were slim. Wilmer might be the best tracker in the world, but he couldn't follow over rock, especially not after Slocum had worked diligently to erase his tracks.

"I reckon I could take a while off from my traveling, since you're so kind to let me ride along like this. There's nowhere for me to get a new horse."

"There's not, is there?" Claudia looked around, as if seeing the country for the first time. Her violet eyes darted about as she took in the details of the steep hills far off on either side of the valley. The area with the green valley looked less like her painting than the rocky canyon Slocum had taken getting here.

"Did you follow me here?" he asked.

"I wouldn't know how," she said, and this carried a ring of sincerity that convinced Slocum her sudden appearance was entirely a matter of luck. He just wasn't sure who it was lucky for.

"The canyon I took getting here looked something like your picture, but there were differences," he said. "Did you paint all the played-out mines?"

"Yes," she said a trifle uncertainly.

"Then we ought to press on and see if a branching trail takes us out of the valley and into rockier terrain you might recognize."

"This is pretty land, isn't it?" she said, looking around like a prairie dog popping up to hunt for danger.

"Good grazing for the horses. And I need to soak my feet. There must be a pond somewhere. The stream running through the middle of the valley is nowhere near as inviting as a pond or lake would be."

"It's been forever since I took a bath," she said, brushing back her reddish-brown mop of hair from her face. Slocum saw grimy trails on her cheeks, as if she had been crying and then wiped away the tears.

The horses surged suddenly, forcing Slocum to pull back on the reins. He grinned and said, "They smell water, and I don't think it's the stream. Up ahead's a likely spot for a pond."

They drove around the gentle swell in the valley and looked down on a fair-sized lake fed by the mountain runoff. Slocum expertly guided the team down the slope until they came up on the shore of a lake so large he could hardly see the far side.

"At last," Claudia said, heaving a deep sigh that caught Slocum's eye. The way her blouse rose and fell so delightfully set him to thinking of other things—like the kiss she had given him back at the Rio Grande.

"Can you take care of the horses, John?"

"I'll stake them out and let them graze," he said. "They've earned it. Then I'll scout the area, just to be on the safe side."

"Oh, the outlaws. I had forgotten about them." Claudia looked worried, then glanced toward the lake. "Should I . . . ?"

"Go on. I'll stand guard," he said.

"You're a dear," she said, giving him another kiss. This time it was only a peck on the cheek, and then she hopped to the ground, looking for a spot to undress. Slocum unhitched the team and found a decent spot for them that would keep both horses busy cropping grass for hours. Then he grabbed a rifle and went hunting.

For men.

A half hour later he had found no trace of the owlhoots who had ambushed him and left him for dead. The wildlife around the lake was active, telling him that things were as normal as could be. He listened to the swallowtails and the distant hunting cry of a half-dozen Harris's hawks as he returned to the buckboard. He dropped his rifle in the back and jumped up to take one last look around.

An army could have been advancing and he would have missed it. All Slocum could see was Claudia frolicking joyously in the lake. The sunlight caught her bare white skin and turned it to pure alabaster. But no hard rock had ever been so warmly inviting to the touch. He felt himself responding to the sight of her bare breasts bobbing to the surface of the lake as she floated on her back, legs scissoring slowly in the water to reveal even more delights. Claudia began reaching up over her head and backstroking toward the shallows. With a sudden flip that revealed the delicious curve of her buttocks and the sleek lines of her body and legs, she reversed direction and swam languidly away from the shoreline.

Slocum tried to avert his eyes. It wasn't right to spy on the lovely woman, yet he couldn't force himself to turn away. She was too lovely. Water glistened on her flesh, and the occasional glimpse of the coppery fleece nestled between her legs made Slocum even harder.

She swam so innocently, a child of nature, pure and unsullied. When she saw him staring, Slocum started to jump down from the wagon.

"Sorry," he said. "I didn't mean to stare."

"Well, I hope you're sorry, John. I don't want you to stare."

"Of course not."

"I want you in the water with me. Naked. Naked and hard."

"What?" She always surprised him, and this took him by storm.

"Are you deaf or just a eunuch? Get in here! Now!"

Her speech had always been hesitant, as if she fought to find the right words. Not now. Slocum stripped off his gun belt and tossed it into the rear of the wagon. As he walked to the edge of the lake, he worked on the buttons holding his shirt and jeans, then sat heavily to pull off his boots and finish shucking off his clothing.

"I was right," Claudia cried in triumph. "You *do* want me!"

"I certainly do," Slocum said, wading into the cold water. He felt himself beginning to shrink as he began swimming.

"You're going to have to work for it," she said. "Catch me!" As agile as a river otter, Claudia flipped over in the water and began swimming powerfully.

She was a strong swimmer. Slocum was faster and had more incentive. He caught her ten yards out from the shore. His fingers curled around her slippery ankle and stopped her powerful scissors kick. She tried to escape, but he dived underwater and came up behind her, pulling her firmly into his body.

His manhood had been flagging because of the cold water. The warmth afforded when he thrust himself between her firm half-moons sent a jolt of such carnal intensity through him and made him think he'd never be limp again. His hands circled her body and came to rest on her firm breasts. He caught the already hard red nips atop each mound of flesh and began toying with them. Claudia sighed and leaned back in the water, pressing her body into his.

They fit together perfectly. He continued to massage one breast as if it were a lump of pliant dough with one hand, and let the other slip slowly across her belly—and lower. The woman gasped when his finger burrowed between her nether lips and invaded her.

"Oh, oh, John, yes," she sobbed out. They floated on the water, locked together like this for several minutes. Slocum explored her body, and she wiggled and twitched delightfully against him, but neither could tolerate the situation forever. They both wanted more.

Slocum's body slipped lower in the water, and then rose beneath her as she spread her legs in a wide vee. He sputtered when she caught his steely shaft and guided it directly into the heated interior where his finger had romped earlier. Slocum was surrounded by warm, moist female flesh that squeezed down on his entire length so delightfully that he could have died happy then and there. He tried to move his hand over her sleek body again, but found that she clutched him too tightly and refused to let go.

With the waves gently tossing them about, Slocum found himself moving in and out of her most intimate recess in a maddeningly slow fashion. He began arching his back and relaxing, accentuating the moves. He slid farther out and plunged deeper with every wave now. When Claudia started moving counter to his stroking, power was added to their watery coupling.

Faster and faster they strove together, until Claudia slammed herself down into the curve of his groin and let out a long, loud cry of release. This forced Slocum deeper underwater, and it took him a few seconds of sputtering to get back up. They had drifted apart, but Claudia was already repositioning herself.

"That was so . . . intense," she breathed heavily. "Now it's your turn."

"Don't shortchange yourself," Slocum said as her legs locked around his waist. She fitted herself around his hard shaft and began bucking up and down. Clinging together, face-to-face this time, kissing passionately, hips levering back and forth until both of them felt the ultimate in human release.

This time they drifted apart, floating on their backs, exhausted from their amorous coupling.

Slocum paddled over and looked at Claudia closely. He would never have thought so much passion could be locked up in her seemingly hesitant body.

"That's about the best way of taking a bath I've ever heard of," he told her.

"It'd better be something you've heard of and not done before," she said primly. "At least not often. You *were* awfully good at it. Have you had practice?"

"Inspiration," Slocum said, swimming closer. He kissed her clumsily as they floated in the lake. "I had incredible inspiration."

He grunted when he felt her fingers working down his belly and grabbing hold of his flaccid organ.

"You want more inspiration?" she asked.

"Not in the water. It's cold."

"It's warm in the sun, stretched out on the grass," she said.

He raced her for the shore. Claudia beat him there and was already on her back, knees bent and open in wanton greeting, when he got there.

7

Slocum sat patiently on a boulder looking back along the trail they had taken getting into another canyon—one that looked identical to another they had traveled the day before. He kept his rifle close at hand, just in case he needed it, although they hadn't seen any other riders. The last human life Slocum had seen, other than the delightful Claudia Peterson, had been the pair of road agents who had shot Pack's horse out from under him. This lack of humanity suited him just fine and left him more time alone with Claudia.

He looked down on where she stood, paintbrush in hand, dabbing at a drawing. For some reason, she had the completed painting set up on a rock where she could look at it and then glance up into the distance where the spent mines dotted the hillsides like some ugly pox. Now and then she would move the completed painting, tip it, shift its position, and then return to her other sketch. Slocum didn't pretend to understand how an artist worked, but this struck him as peculiar.

He shrugged it off. The nights were warm and passionate with her, and the days sometimes were also. Claudia had more locked up inside her than he'd expected. It made spending a few more days—or weeks—driving her around the Sangre de Cristo Mountains worthwhile. Sooner or later he would tire of her or she of him, and it would be time to get a horse and ride on alone. Until then, Slocum was like a bear with a limitless honeycomb.

"John!" Claudia threw down her paintbrush in disgust and stood, hands on flaring hips, with a sour expression on her lovely face. "This isn't right. It's just not right. I thought it was, but . . ."

He slid down the rock and landed hard. Brushing himself off, he dropped the rifle barrel into the crook of his left arm as he went to study her sketch. It contained the barest hint of what lay in front of her.

"It's not right. Just not right," she said. "We need to find another place. See?" She pointed to the completed painting. "There are three mine shafts up and to the right. Here are only two. Two, and I don't know what that is."

Slocum squinted into the sun where Claudia pointed.

"Looks like a premature explosion. Might be a miner detonated it prematurely, or hit rock too hard to blast with Giant powder, so he moved lower on the slope."

"I don't know anything about that," Claudia said. "I do know we have to find another spot like this, only with *three* mines in precisely those locations." She tapped the painting again.

"What's so important about finding the precise spot? One canyon looks like another to me."

"No!" The flare of anger lit her face. Then she blushed and looked away, mumbling, "Sorry, John. I am so frustrated. Nothing is going right."

He came up behind her and put his arms around her quaking body.

"Nothing?"

"Oh, not that, not you, not you and me. I meant *this*! The drawing is not going well at all. I have to find the precise spot . . . for inspiration."

"I don't inspire you?"

"You exhaust me," Claudia said, turning and tipping her face to his. She kissed him lightly, then with more passion. "Want to exhaust me some more right now?"

He did.

"This might be the place," Claudia said excitedly. She bounced up and down on the hard wooden seat next to Slocum, her face flushed and her eyes glowing. "There? See the mines? Three of them in the right positions! Oh, John, I've found it. I just know it."

• "You're mighty excited just to be back where you've been before," he said. Slocum didn't understand Claudia or her reaction. To him, this canyon looked like the one they had just left. He shielded his eyes with his hand and studied the slopes on either side, counted mine shafts, and then realized he had been here before too. On his way from Las Vegas, he had come through this canyon on his roundabout path to Taos.

"This is the place where I can make a perfect picture. I feel it, John, I just feel it in my bones."

"Nice bones too to feel," Slocum said. Before, Claudia would have risen to his comment. Not now. She was too engrossed in pointing out various landmarks, hardly more than piles of rock and discarded rubble from deep in the mines.

"Drive in that direction," she said in a tone Slocum had not heard before. She was ordering him around like a servant in a way that rankled. He almost balked, then did as she wanted. His curiosity was beginning to run wild. If he stayed quiet and let Claudia have her way, he would find what excited her so much.

He guided the buckboard down a rocky road, and stopped only when she grabbed his arm in a steely grip.

"Here. Stop here." She jumped down and grabbed her easel and the finished painting. She looked around, then hiked up a low hill.

"You want a blank canvas or your paints?" Slocum called after her. It was as if Claudia didn't hear him. He saw her struggling to get to the top of the knoll, where she put up her easel and began turning it this way and that to align the picture with the actual landscape.

Slocum stared at her in wonder. Everything else had disappeared for her in a flash of recognition. But what had she recognized? Slocum turned from Claudia to the side of the mountain where three open mines gaped. From the look of the entire area, it had played out a long time back. There might be coal here, but the original miners had come for gold and silver and had found precious little. Down south in the Sandia Mountains, the coal mines fed a steady stream of the black rock to the railroad in Lamy. There was almost as much money in coal as there would have been in silver, but not in these mountains.

He jumped down and began unloading enough supplies for a two-day stay. From the way Claudia had worked before, sketching and moving on the same day, he thought two days would be all she required to finish her painting. He scratched his head and wondered about that. She had never let him get a good gander at the painting, but it looked to be complete. She dabbed paint around the very edges of it, but never changed anything important. He shrugged it off. He wasn't an artist, and knew nothing about what she wanted to depict.

Making a small fire afforded him fresh coffee. He had finished a second cup by the time she came down from her perch atop the knoll, still flushed and anxious.

"Oh, John, this is the place. I've found it."

"Again."

"What? Oh, yes, I've found it again. You brought me straight to it."

"Seems like we've spent the better part of a week meandering through these mountains. That's hardly coming straight to it," he said.

"I could have spent a lifetime if you hadn't already seen this particular canyon and located it for me. You really rode through here when you left Las Vegas?"

"Ran across a couple riders near this spot," Slocum said. "Might have been the outlaws who shot my horse. This is dangerous territory."

"It's magical territory," she said rapturously.

"Have some dinner," he said. "I fixed the coffee and can rustle up grub in a few minutes."

"I want to explore the area," she said. "Now. Before it gets too dark."

"The mountains and mines will be here in the morning, same as they've been here for years."

"The light will be different. That's important to artists. Light."

Slocum got to his feet.

"I'll go along, just to keep you safe."

"Don't be silly. Fix dinner. I won't be more than a few minutes. Half hour at the most."

"Don't get lost. You'd be surprised how easy it is getting lost out here."

"I've firsthand experience with that," she said. Seeing his skeptical expression, she added, "In forests. Back in Illinois. It is quite easy to wander off and lose direction in a forest. I learned how to make my way."

"Doesn't help much out here," Slocum said. "The miners stripped the trees off the slopes within months for supports and roofing in the mines. There's nothing but bare rock left."

"That makes it all the easier," she said.

"Makes what easier?"

"Why, finding the right place to do another painting," she said. Again Slocum wanted to warn her against playing poker. Her face had *LIE!* written all over it.

"Don't be too long," he said.

"I won't. I want to get back and eat. I'm famished. And then we can . . . celebrate."

"That big a day for you?" Slocum asked.

"It will be if we celebrate enough," she said coyly. Blowing him a kiss, Claudia hurried away, going downslope toward an arroyo running through the canyon.

Slocum fixed the grub and nibbled at it uneasily, not sure why he was not anticipating her return. A lovely woman, excited about finding what she had sought, willing to share a blanket with him—why didn't he feel better? Slocum poked at the food he had fried up in the skillet, then set it down. The sky was turning dark fast. When the sun set in the mountains, night fell with a speed unknown out on the plains—or in forests.

"Claudia!" he called. "Come and get it. Dinner!" Slocum listened hard, but heard nothing. He reached down and touched the butt of his six-shooter. Twilight was a dangerous time to be wandering around. He hadn't seen any trace of cougar, but this was when they hunted. Nothing else was dangerous enough to matter, unless a wolf pack roved the canyon. Slocum hadn't seen traces of the wild animals earlier today or when he had ridden this canyon before, but that didn't mean it wasn't part of their range.

He called again, and didn't get a reply. Putting the skillet aside, he got to his feet and followed the game trail Claudia had taken. It turned steep fast, and then veered away from the arroyo where he thought she had been going. Nothing showed she had left the trail.

Slocum picked his way along with increasing caution, both because the darkness prevented him from seeing where he walked and because of an eerie feeling that something was terribly wrong. He saw no reason for Claudia to simply vanish. Slocum drew his six-shooter and placed each foot carefully to avoid dislodging stones and making even the slightest noise. As he made his way along the game trail, he strained to hear what might be ahead.

A strange moaning sound came to him. At first he thought it was the breeze gusting through a crack in the rocks around him; then he realized there wasn't a breath of wind blowing. He refrained from calling out to see if this was Claudia making the sound.

His cautious walking saved him from falling headlong into a dark chasm in the middle of the path. The game trail simply ended on one side of the hole and kept going on the other. Slocum guessed that miners had cored out the rock under the trail, weakening it to the point where it finally fell into the shaft. The entire area must be a honeycomb of tunnels and shafts, with only the few poking out of the mountainsides visible.

Slocum dropped to his knees and cocked his head to one side. He heard the moaning again, and this time he knew it was human.

"Claudia!"

"John? That you?"

"What happened? Did you stumble into the pit?"

"I didn't see it. Oh, I hurt!"

"Did you break any bones?"

More moans and then. "I don't think so. It hurts to stand, but that's because I bruised . . . myself."

Slocum held down a laugh. He guessed what portion of her anatomy Claudia had bruised and that she was too discreet to name it. His imagination showed her rubbing her rump and moaning some more.

"Get me out. I don't think there's any other way out of here," she said, her voice stronger.

"I'll have to get a rope and pull you out. There's no way I can climb down in the dark without being stranded with you."

"Hurry, John. It's cold and damp down here."

"Is there water seeping in?" Slocum knew miners often drowned by blasting and digging through rock and releasing underground rivers. If a stream had been released, Claudia could drown in a few minutes.

"No, it's just damp. And cold. I'm shivering, John. Get me out of here!"

"I'll fetch the rope and then get something warm into you."

"Is that a promise?"

Slocum laughed as he backtracked to their camp to get his rope. All he needed to do was drop the loop down, have Claudia slip her arms through it, and then pull her up. From the way her voice echoed, she wasn't farther down than fifteen feet. Still, she was lucky she hadn't hurt herself seriously taking a spill down a distance like that.

As he reached the camp, Slocum's hand flashed to his six-gun. He froze. Upslope he heard a horse neighing and its rider mumbling constantly. Slocum left the game trail and worked his way up through the rocks until he reached another trail higher on the mountainside.

A quick sniff warned Slocum whom he was spying on.

"Wilmer," he said, making the name into a curse. The bounty hunter was either lucky, or about the best tracker Slocum had ever come across. At the moment, Slocum was willing to bet on lucky since Wilmer had missed the camp and its dying cook fire, passing it on his way to the south.

Slocum scrambled the rest of the way to the trail and stood behind the bounty hunter. He drew his pistol and aimed, then lowered it. He wasn't a backshooter. He had no quarrel with Wilmer other than wanting the man to believe he wasn't Neale.

Grumbling noisily, Wilmer dismounted and turned from his horse to take a leak. A wild plan came to Slocum. He acted before he could talk himself out of such foolhardiness. He thrust his six-shooter back into its holster, then walked fast to where Wilmer urinated.

Slocum shoved the man hard, sending him flailing into a patch of prickly pear cactus. Before the bounty hunter's horse could rear, Slocum vaulted into the saddle and put his heels to the frightened horse's flanks. He galloped off in the dark, not even considering how easy it would be for the horse to break a leg—or worse. It might fall into an open mining shaft like the one Claudia had tumbled down. Horse and rider falling fifteen feet meant death for both. But Slocum wanted to get rid of Wilmer without killing him, if he could, and this presented a good chance of working.

After Wilmer's outraged shouts died down because of distance and the horse began to tire, Slocum eased back, and finally brought the horse to a stop. He looked around in the dark and finally saw a cholla. Sliding from the saddle, he held the reins tightly to keep the horse from bolting.

"Hate to do this to you, but I want you to run for a good, long time," Slocum said. He plucked a cane of cholla with nasty, long spines. Lifting the saddle blanket, Slocum laid the cholla down on bare horseflesh, then cinched down the saddle to hold it in place under the blanket. The horse let out a squeal that sounded human and raced off.

Slocum got off the trail and worked his way higher, then started back toward his camp. Almost a half hour of walking brought him even with Wilmer on the trail below. The bounty hunter cursed constantly and walked with a curious bowlegged, rolling gait Slocum considered more appropriate for a sailor just off his ship. He almost laughed when he figured out what had happened when Wilmer had fallen. Slocum was glad he didn't have the viciously long prickly pear spines in that portion of *his* anatomy.

He kept on until he returned to the buckboard and checked their supplies. Slocum was glad to see that Wilmer had bypassed the camp entirely. Grabbing his rope from his saddle stashed in the rear of the wagon, he set out on the trail to get Claudia out of the pit. Wilmer might be back in a day or two or he might return sooner, but whichever it was, Slocum needed to let Claudia know her time here was going to be limited—or that it was time for him to move on alone. Wilmer was not going to give up, especially after what happened to him this night.

8

"Grab the rope and loop it around you," Slocum called down to Claudia. "I'll pull you out."

"Wait a few minutes, John."

"What? Are you hurt? You said you were all right."

"I was getting mad at you for taking so long. It's been hours," she shouted up at him. "Then I found something."

"What?" Slocum turned wary. She had the sound of a miner who had come across a fleck of fool's gold. Excitement and hope and visions of fortune mingled to make her sure the world was going to change for her.

"I . . . I'll tell you later. Let me work a few more—got it!"

"Can I pull you up now?" Slocum's patience was fading fast. He doubted Wilmer was going to return tonight, or for a day or two maybe, but the bounty hunter had a single-minded determination that might not be snuffed until a bullet ripped through his heart. Slocum wanted to avoid that and get into Colorado, away from him and Marshal Hanks and everyone else who thought he was named Neale.

"Yes, I have the rope around my waist. Pull up."

Slocum took a turn around a rock spire, then began pulling, using his legs to add to the power of the lift. Claudia was a small thing and easily picked up, but pulling her out of the pit required a lot more strength because of the ragged edges to the pit. Tugging, grunting, Slocum finally saw the top of her head appear at the edge of the pit. He yanked hard until she surged upward and flopped facedown on the game trail.

"Whew, you are quite a haul," Slocum said. She looked up at him in disgust, then her expression changed. She reached down to her waistband and pulled out what looked like a short stick.

"See? I found it! Or one like it!"

"What is it?" Slocum reached for the stick in her hand, but she jerked it away.

"It's mine," she said, obviously wishing she hadn't shown him her treasure.

"I've got something to tell you."

"I have to go back down," she said, not listening to him. "There's more. I know it. I don't know how it ended up there, but I'm so lucky!"

"Not so lucky," Slocum said, helping her to her feet and dusting her off. He quickly related all that had happened on his way back to the camp, how he had lured Wilmer away and what was likely to happen.

"Oh, pish," she said. "Why would he want to come back? He never saw you. It could have been anyone who did that to him."

"Then he'll want to plug 'anyone' before getting back on my trail. He is like the wind. He doesn't stop and keeps coming, sneaking in through any crevice he finds to chill your bones. I want to hightail it north and leave him as far behind as I can. Otherwise, we're going to shoot it out."

"Oh, don't be so dramatic. It wouldn't come to that," Claudia said confidently. "I can go back down at first light. I know where to look, but I might need a torch. You can make me a torch, can't you, so I can look around better down there?" She glanced over her shoulder in the direction of the shaft, making it apparent to Slocum that she hadn't understood his concern over Wilmer's return.

Back in camp Claudia was too excited to eat, but their lovemaking carried a frantic release that reflected more her overwhelming thrill at finding a small stick of wood at the bottom of the pit than being with Slocum.

"Is there any other way to get in?" she asked as she peered over the lip of the shaft where she had fallen in the night before. "I don't want to have you lower me down there if there is."

"I tried to find the mouth of the mine where this stope was excavated, but couldn't," Slocum said. "Most of the mines weren't well built, and the roofs collapsed. Getting into any of the ones remaining open is mighty dangerous."

"Then you'll have to lower me."

"Is it necessary?" Slocum wondered at her eagerness to end up where she had been screaming bloody murder to get out the day before. "What do you expect to find down there?"

"I'd let you go," Claudia went on, not hearing him, "but I could never pull you back up. And you said that smelly bounty-hunter fellow might return. You should keep watch up here. Getting caught at the bottom of the pit isn't a good idea."

"No, it isn't," Slocum said dryly. He uncoiled the rope and handed Claudia the looped end. She slipped it around her waist without an instant of hesitation, then moved to the pit, looked down, and shuddered before saying, "Lower me now, John. I'll be back before you know it."

"I'll drop the torch when you get to the bottom."

He lowered her, then lit the torch, let it sputter and got rid of most of the smoky ignition, then dropped it. He saw Claudia clumsily catch it. Then the light was muted as she fell to her knees and began examining the rock fall that had sealed off the stope from the main drift. The black haze rising from the shaft like smoke from a chimney worried Slocum. Wilmer ought to have run his horse to ground by now and would backtrack pronto. This was a beacon to a man with nothing but reward—and vengeance—on his mind.

A loud cry echoed up the shaft. Slocum poked his head over the edge and saw Claudia holding up another stick, clucking in delight. She waved the torch about and called, "Haul me up. I've got it!"

Slocum told her to drop the torch, then began pulling. In minutes Claudia was once more in the fresh clean air and away from the sooty torch. Her face was smudged with black, and her usually clean clothing had become filthy. She paid no heed to any of that, which had occupied her so previously. She held up a whole paintbrush in triumph and waved it around so that it caught the sunlight. As far as Slocum could tell, the bristles were chewed off by rats and the wood handle was battered.

"Why is that so important?"

"It . . . it is, John. I haven't been entirely honest with you up till now."

Slocum stared at her. She had been lying and he hadn't realized it? When she blushed at the drop of a hat and always looked guilty when she was telling even the smallest fib?

"I didn't draw that painting—the finished one. My father did. He came out here months and months ago and—" A catch came to her voice and tears welled in her violet eyes. "He was killed. I don't know what happened. Not exactly, but the painting arrived in Chicago and I wanted to find the place where he did it. This was his last work and I feel such a connection—I want to feel even more."

"This was the last place he was alive?"

"I think that's true," Claudia said, wiping at her tears. "This is one of his brushes. I don't know how it ended up down there with the other one, but it did. I recognize it as his favorite brush."

"Favorite?"

"Oh, yes, John!" She looked so bright and cheerful now that the tears might have been years in the past. "All artists have one or two special brushes. This was my papa's."

"How can you tell?"

"Let's get back to camp. I want to work on my own again, now that I have this for inspiration. It . . . it'll make everything so much easier for me."

"You know where he's buried?"

"Not around here, I suspect. But this was probably the last place he worked. That's why he sent me the painting."

Slocum kicked himself for not twigging instantly to the problem with Claudia's story. If her father had died here, it wasn't too likely he would have been able to send her the finished painting. He had to have reached some town with an express office. But that didn't explain why he had left his brushes behind.

"You think he dropped the brushes down the pit on purpose?"

"Why'd he—oh!" Claudia turned and gave him a big kiss.

"Not that I minded that, but what's got you all hot and bothered?"

"I missed a clue," she said. Claudia quickly rushed on. "My papa was always one to put things into his paintings to make them his very own. I mean more than the style or the color selection or the brush stroke. He put little things in."

Back in camp she went to the painting, carefully pulled it from its box, and pointed to the bottom of the painting.

"There it is. How could I have missed it?"

Slocum saw what appeared to be shadows, but they crossed in an impossible way. If Claudia's father had painted what he had seen, the sun would have cast the shadows in the same direction, not in an X. He checked the distances and locations of the three mines on the distant slope and decided she was right. The spot indicated on the painting was about where the shaft dropped down fifteen feet from the game trail.

"Why'd he want you to know where he had tossed old paintbrushes?"

"Keepsakes," she said without hesitation. Claudia took the painting back, grabbed her easel and the sketch she had been working on, and said, "I'll be working. Oh, I feel the muse touching my shoulder, guiding my hand."

"Muse?"

"Inspiration, John, I am so inspired. I can hardly contain myself." She kissed him again before he could ask any more questions, and hurried up the slope to begin her work again. Slocum got a hollow feeling in his belly. More was going on than Claudia was telling him. None of her story about her pa made any sense, except the part about someone else rather than her doing the painting. Her sketches were decent, but showed none of the skill in the landscape.

Slocum oiled his Colt Navy and Winchester and made sure both were fully loaded. If he tangled with Wilmer again, he knew that lead would fly. When he finished, Slocum hiked up the hill to see how Claudia was doing. To his surprise, she was nowhere to be seen.

"Claudia!"

"Over here, John. Don't look. I had to answer a call to nature."

Slocum wasn't inclined to look at her because he saw how she had left the second paintbrush resting against the painting. A small arrow had been drawn on the handle at an angle. And on the painting itself was a slender cigar-shaped marking. On impulse, he picked up the brush and pressed it into the spot. The arrow on the brush's handle pointed back down the valley in the direction they had come to get this far.

"John," Claudia said, coming up behind him. "I wish you hadn't seen that."

"It's a treasure map," he said in disgust. If he'd been

given a dollar for every map promising immense wealth, he would have been rich—from the dollars, not the hidden treasures. Hunting down such buried fortunes racked up a huge body count and damned little gold.

"In a manner of speaking, I suppose it is," she said. "I owe you so much. I wouldn't have gotten from the pit without you and that's where I found the brush and—"

"How'd your pa come by the treasure?"

"I . . . I don't know. The note with the painting said there was a fabulous amount of gold hidden and that the painting was the way to find it."

"We've got to get out of here soon," Slocum said. "The bounty hunter will be back before you know it."

"But the gold is around here. That's what the map says," Claudia pleaded. "We need to go back up the canyon, in the direction where we came. If we go back toward that valley, with the lake where you and I . . ."

Slocum knew she was making a blatant appeal to him. It fell on deaf ears, but he couldn't abandon her, nor could he steal one of her horses to get away from Wilmer. Like it or not, he was stuck with following this rainbow to its bitter end.

"How do you know where it's supposed to be?"

"I . . . I don't know for sure, but there's got to be a clue in the painting. We found the shaft where the paintbrush was hidden."

"Discarded," Slocum corrected.

"Once I put it on the painting in the proper spot, we know the direction to go."

"Is the length of the arrow some indicator of how far to go?"

"What do you mean?" Her eyes were as wide as could be with wonder.

"Is there anything on the map—the painting," he corrected himself, "that shows proportions? Maybe the arrow being an inch long means we ought to go a mile in that direction. Or a hundred feet."

"A proportion, yes," Claudia said. "That makes sense. I can measure it against the size of the mine openings. Or something close by. The brush itself!"

Slocum let her fiddle and fuss over the dimensions while he worried over how near Wilmer might be by now. The bounty hunter was too determined to give up, and there had been plenty of time for him to get back. Slocum considered shooting him and taking his horse, but horse thieving was worse than murder. He had to do something to keep out of jail—or worse. Having a rope around his neck and an open trapdoor under his feet wasn't to his liking any more than tangling with Wilmer.

"I've got it, John. Two miles back that way. Oh, yes, come on, let's go."

"You go. I'll catch up with you."

"What is it?"

"I'll wait for the bounty hunter," he said. "There's no reason to let him know why you're out here," he said, giving the one argument that would work best with the woman. Claudia nodded knowingly in agreement. "Get going right now," he told her. "And don't worry about hiding your tracks. In this rocky country, it wouldn't work too well. Just don't hide too good when you find the right spot or I might not be able to find you again."

"All right," she said, then looked up sharply. "Oh, you. You're kidding me. There's no way you could miss me."

"Go," he said. He let her kiss him, but Claudia's mind was already on digging up the treasure her father had left behind. Slocum grabbed his rifle from the back of the buckboard and hiked up the hill where she had put her easel. From here he could watch as she drove northward, as well as see the trail where Wilmer had to ride.

Claudia had barely gotten out of sight when Slocum saw the relentless bounty hunter riding along. The man looked to be in pain. This gave Slocum a small bit of pleasure because he knew why every bounce and jostle caused such discomfort to the bounty hunter, but even the cactus spines in his privates didn't deter Wilmer.

Slocum looked for a better spot to get the drop on the bounty hunter, and found it quickly. He scooted down the hill and walked quickly toward the pit where Claudia had found the brush. Just above it on the hillside provided good cover, and Wilmer would ride along the game trail. If he fell into the shaft, so much the better for Slocum, but counting on that happening was a fool's game.

He levered a round into the rifle's chamber and waited for less than ten minutes for the bounty hunter to ride into view.

"Stop right there," Slocum called when it was apparent Wilmer wasn't going to tumble headlong into the pit.

"Neale!"

"I'm not Neale," Slocum said wearily. "I want you to give up following me. I'm not the outlaw you want."

"Are too. I got a good memory fer pitchurs, and that's as ugly a face as I can remember seein'!"

Slocum stood, swung easily, aimed, and fired. Wilmer jumped in the saddle, then checked himself for holes. Slocum had not shot him in cold blood. The bounty hunter turned to see what Slocum already had.

"Outlaws!" Slocum cried. He recognized the lead rider as the one named Dusty. He fired steadily and brought Dusty out of the saddle with a decent shot so the rider fell heavily to the ground. He didn't move once he flopped down onto the dirt. Three other road agents crowded close behind and began flinging lead all over.

"Land o' Goshen," cried Wilmer. He swung around, ignoring the bullets whining past him as he looked from Slocum to the outlaws and back. "Yer right. Yer not Neale. *That's* Neale!"

Slocum blinked when he saw the man who had ridden directly behind Dusty. He thought he was looking in a mirror. He started to shoot Neale, but Wilmer was already firing wildly. As tenacious as the mountain man was as a tracker, he was a piss-poor marksman and scattered the outlaws rather than hitting any of them.

Wilmer got his horse turned around and charged straight into the guns trained on him. Wilmer had to lead a charmed life because not a single bullet found him.

"I'll git you, you varmint," he shouted as he rode straight for Neale.

Slocum stopped firing, and slid down the slope in time to catch the reins of Dusty's horse as it tried to bolt and run away from the gunfire. He swung into the saddle and stayed low as he left the bounty hunter and the outlaws far behind to shoot it out. No matter what happened, Slocum figured he was safe.

The outlaws didn't know who he was and probably didn't care. And Wilmer was content with actually spotting Neale and going after him.

Slocum stayed low and galloped away, looking forward to finding Claudia Peterson again. He doubted her pa had left behind any gold, and Slocum knew a better way to hunt for treasure with her.

9

Claudia Peterson had traveled more than a couple miles.
Slocum overtook her back in the meadow where she had
come across him earlier when he had been on foot. He
slowed his headlong retreat and looked down at the
woman. She barely acknowledged him since she was so
busy setting up her easel with its painting and the brush.

"Wilmer and some outlaws are shooting it out," Slocum
said.

"Then they won't bother us," Claudia said, not even
looking up. She turned the brush around until it fit in the
proper place, then dragged her finger over the wood, trac-
ing the arrow and checking with the painting. Her shoulders slumped as she looked up. "I don't know what to do
now. The painting was of the mines back in the canyon, but
the clues lead here."

Slocum considered simply getting his gear and leaving
her to the hunt. He doubted she would find so much as a
corroded penny out here, but in spite of having a horse now
and being able to travel without her, he knew she was in
deep trouble if the outlaws found her.

He dismounted and went to the easel. A bit of estima-
tion showed she was right about distance and direction.

Claudia was also right about the lack of direction now that they had left the spot where the painting had been made.

"What's that?" Slocum pointed to a small stand of trees at the bottom of the painting.

"Trees. So?"

"So the entire canyon had been cut clean as a freshly shaved preacher to use as the support beams in the mines. There might have been trees in the canyon at one time, but not now."

"You're right! This has to mean that the treasure is in a grove of trees. But where? There're nothing but trees!"

She spun in a complete circle, causing her skirts to billow out and show a bit of ankle. Slocum took a deep breath and settled his emotions. He had to use his head, not other parts of his anatomy.

"Your pa had something in mind. You're the one who can figure it out." Slocum licked his lips and considered riding on again. Then he imagined he heard distant gunfire and smelled pungent gunsmoke, and knew he couldn't leave Claudia behind. The horse he had taken from the dead outlaw gave him too many options, and they got in the way of what he knew was right. He couldn't ride away from Claudia until he was certain she was safe.

"You're right. I came this far. I can't give up. Not when . . . when he wanted me to have the gold."

"Why didn't he just come out and say where the gold was hidden?"

"Papa was always very secretive. He and . . . the rest of my family. We never shared much," Claudia said contritely. Then she smiled. "But I won't mind sharing with you, John. Anything."

"You're offering me some of your hidden gold?"

"For all you've done so far, you deserve it. I would have been a moldering corpse at the bottom of that shaft without you."

"I've got to tell you this and hope you understand," he

said. He took a deep breath. "Those outlaws Wilmer is tackling will probably kill him. There are too many for even a lucky, tough galoot like Wilmer to get the better of."

"So?"

"The outlaws are probably after the gold too. If it is worth you coming all the way from Chicago, it's worth their time to kill a few people—including you—to get it."

"They can't do that! It's mine! Papa wanted it for me. He *owed* me."

Slocum didn't bother asking why Claudia thought that. She did and that was good enough to keep her hunting, no matter how many road agents came sweeping through this peaceful valley.

"I don't know if the outlaws have a hideout around here. Probably do. It might be that they know nothing about the gold. Was it stolen?" A dozen possibilities ran through Slocum's mind. The gold mines dotting the region might not all have come up barren of ore. A shipment from even one decent mine would provide a small fortune to whoever stole it. Or there might have been a stagecoach robbery, or the cavalry could have lost a payroll. That explained the campground Slocum had found and the large number of soldiers that had bivouacked there. Claudia's pa had stolen a shipment and, true to military thinking, they had locked the barn door after the horse was gone. No other horse could escape, and no new payroll shipment could be hijacked without facing a couple dozen soldiers, but the robbery had gone unpunished and the gold had never been recovered. There were other possibilities where the gold might have come from, and none of them entailed honest hard work on Mr. Peterson's part.

"Stolen?" Claudia sounded unsure. "I don't think so. Papa was an artist, not a bank robber. He wouldn't know how to steal. That was why we were always as poor as church mice."

Slocum doubted Claudia was being square with him, but he didn't press the point. The anticipation of Neale and his gang riding up made Slocum edgy.

"We'll look for an hour or two and if we don't find it, we move on," he said.

"No!"

"Let me finish," Slocum said. "We stop hunting for a spell, go back to Taos or just camp for a week or so, and let the outlaws move on."

"You said they might have a hideout here."

"I'll scout the area to be sure. If they do, the marshal over in Las Vegas might find it useful knowing where it is. I get word to him, he brings a posse and arrests or chases off the outlaws, then we have all the time in the world to hunt for your pa's treasure."

"You wouldn't run off?"

"Why'd I do a thing like that with the promise of so much treasure?" he asked. She looked angry. Slocum grabbed her by the arm and spun her around into his arms so he could kiss her. "There's real treasure," he said. "And I didn't even have to dig for it."

"A shame," Claudia said. "I enjoy the way you plow."

"You are quite a handful, aren't you?" Slocum laughed as he released her. Claudia swung away and ended up facing the painting, frowning and intent on deciphering its hidden message. If there even was one there. Slocum had his doubts about this being a map, much less a map to a fortune in gold Claudia did not know even existed. From what she said, her pa wasn't the most likely sort to even stumble across such wealth.

"If these are trees," she said, "might be the number or type of tree means something."

Slocum squinted at the painting. Then he stood and looked around.

"White bark means either aspen or birch. This meadow's too low for them to be aspen. There's a stand of birch trees." He pointed. A quick count matched the number with what the painting showed. His heart began to hammer a little faster. This was more than coincidence. Seven distinctively placed birch trees deliberately itemized on the painting.

"Where would he hide the treasure?" Slocum asked. "In the grove of trees?"

"I don't know, John," she said. "Let's go look. Something might suggest itself if we poke around enough."

"How long has it been since you got the painting? If it hasn't been more than a month, the dirt might still be loose over the spot where the gold's hidden."

"So you think I'm telling the truth now?"

"I never doubted what you believe," Slocum said. "I'm still not sure about the gold."

"Any dirt would have settled back and packed itself down. It's been more than three months since I got the painting. It took a while for me to leave Chicago."

Slocum heard more in what she was saying than she actually said. Had Claudia left behind a husband or boyfriend? Or had she sneaked away without telling the rest of her family?

"What about your ma?"

Slocum saw he had struck to the heart of the matter.

"She died. I . . . I was nursing her while Papa was out West doing his painting. She succumbed about a month after I got the painting, and it took me two months to get her affairs in order."

"Sorry," Slocum said. It was plausible, but Claudia had lied convincingly to him before, looking as if she was the worst liar in the world and then making it count when she had to put one over on him.

They started walking for the birch grove. Slocum thought hard on why he kept doubting Claudia. It might be that she was simply too good to be true, but he knew it went deeper than that. When it came down to counting chips, Slocum was a good poker player and read the others at the table well. She held back too much from him, masking the deceptions with wide-eyed innocence, for him to feel completely comfortable with her. He doubted she would shoot him in the back, but anything up to that, including swindling him, was fair game.

But just in case, he wasn't going to turn his back on her if she was carrying a gun.

"Seven," she said. "Seven was Papa's favorite number. And he always said it was perfectly formed with fours and threes."

Slocum saw four trees to one side of the small grove and three to the other. The spot directly between the two groups was grassy, but his sharp eyes caught something that gave him pause. A patch of grass looked greener than the surrounding area—and the dimensions of that patch were about what he would expect from a grave.

"This might not be the right place," Slocum said.

"No, no, this is it. I feel it. And here is the spot where I'd put my treasure if I were Papa." She stood directly on the too-green patch, oblivious to its shape and dimensions.

"What happened to your pa?"

"I don't know. I told you. I . . . I suspect he might be dead." Tears welled in her eyes. "Why else would he send the painting and never follow it himself? He didn't even come back for Mama's funeral."

"You think he knew she'd died?"

"I wrote letters."

"Where did you send them?"

"To Santa Fe," she said. "I don't know how long it took him to pick them up. There wasn't an address. I just sent them to him in care of general delivery."

Slocum stared at the ground, hoping he was wrong. He had seen too many graves to doubt it.

"If the gold's not here, where else might it be?"

"John," she said solemnly, "what's wrong? You sound so . . . different."

"Look at the ground where you are standing. The grass is greener and in a rectangle about the size of a grave."

Claudia jumped as if someone had given her a hotfoot. She stared at the grass, then dropped to her knees and ran her fingers a few inches along the boundary between the different shades of green.

"It's been dug up," she said. "You . . . you think it's a grave? My father's buried here?"

"That'd mean he brought someone else to where he had hidden the gold and a swap was made. Him for the gold." Slocum walked around, then added, "There might be something else there, though. Nobody who'd dry-gulch a man to steal his gold would bury him. Better to leave the body out where the animals could get to it."

"Why? Why would that be better?" Claudia was aggrieved now at what he was suggesting.

"Because it's easier," Slocum said. "I'll go get something to dig with. You had a shovel in the wagon."

"I expected to do a fair amount of digging. There's a pickax too. Would that be better for digging in dirt like this?" She reached down and pressed her palm flat against the grass.

Slocum left her and went to the wagon, got in, and drove it to the stand of trees. He took his time rummaging around in the back of the buckboard for the tools so she would have time to herself. Everything he'd said was all guesswork, and he might be completely wrong. But he didn't think so.

Pick over one shoulder and carrying the shovel over the other, he entered the shelter of the birches and tossed the shovel to the ground, favoring the pickax for the preliminary work. He put his gun belt aside and wiped off his hands before getting down to work. Claudia watched from a few feet away, face drawn and anxious.

When he had pulled up the sod, he turned to the shovel and began digging. The dirt turned softer, and he knew it had been turned recently. More carefully, he removed the dirt so he wouldn't damage the corpse he knew was in the grave. When his shovel skidded off something hard, he dropped to his knees and brushed away enough to reveal a shoe.

"There is a body, isn't there?" Claudia was crying openly now.

"It's not your father," Slocum said. "Not unless he's got a mighty small foot."

"What?"

Slocum began digging faster now, moving the dirt away from the body to reveal a woman about Claudia's height and build. It was hard to tell the color of her hair because it was so filthy, and the flesh was drawn back with maggot holes throughout where the worms had burrowed aggressively. Slocum wiped back the last of the dirt from the dead woman's face and couldn't recognize her. She had been buried too long.

But Claudia let out a tiny gasp.

"You know her?"

"Th-that's my sister," she said. Then she fainted.

10

"How do you know it's your sister?"

"That's Maggie," Claudia said. "She's wearing her favorite dress. And the locket. The tiny silver locket. It has a picture of our parents in it." Claudia's hand fluttered like a wounded bird flying in the direction of the open grave. Slocum supported her with his arm around her shoulder. She was pale, but color slowly returned to her cheeks.

"You want the locket as a keepsake?"

"If you don't mind, John. I . . . I couldn't touch her to get it. She was so pretty. Far lovelier than I am!"

Slocum bit his tongue to keep from saying that was no longer true, if it ever had been. He made sure Claudia was able to sit up on her own, then went to the grave and looked down at the body. A closer examination showed what he had missed earlier. There was a small hole between the woman's breasts. She had been shot. From the look of the burned fabric, whoever shot her had done it at close range and the gunpowder spat from the muzzle had set fire to her blouse.

Slocum pushed it back and saw that the hole was good-sized. No belly gun had been used on Maggie Peterson. She had been shot with a .45 or even something larger, though he doubted it was as big as a .50. That would mean she had let someone close in on her with a buffalo rifle and shoot her point-blank. Slocum rolled her half over, bones clattering, and saw the spot where the bullet had exited through her spine. She had died instantly. That told Slocum a little more. Whoever had killed her wasn't after information. She would have been tortured if they hadn't known already what she knew. Her killer had wanted her dead.

He dropped the body back into the grave flat on its back, then worked on the silver locket around her neck. He finally opened the catch and held it in his hand, wondering what Claudia and Maggie's parents looked like. It might help if he knew what her father looked like. Before he could open it, a quick hand snatched it away and closed over it.

"Thank you, John. I could never have beared to take it like you did. She's so . . . dead."

"That's what happens when you get shot close up with a big-caliber gun," he said, trying to shock Claudia into giving him more information. Slocum was reaching the point of needing to know what was going on since his own life might depend on it.

"You end up very dead," Claudia said without emotion. "Like Maggie."

"You want anything else from the grave?"

"What? Oh, no, sorry. I was thinking of growing up together. She was always the daring one, and now she's gone. It isn't right. I want to know who killed her."

"The outlaws up the canyon would be a good bet," Slocum said. "Their leader's named Neale, and he looks a lot like me. It wouldn't surprise me if he wasn't the one who shot your sister."

"Neale," Claudia said, rolling the name over and over like she tasted something unpleasant on her tongue. "I'd actually wondered if you might be Neale when both the marshal and the bounty hunter came looking for you. For

Neale. For—oh, never mind." She turned away and buried her face in her hands, shoulders shaking as she sobbed.

Slocum tossed dirt back over Maggie Peterson until he had a mound built again. He considered finding stone and marking the grave, or at least putting rocks over the dirt to keep the wild animals from digging her up. Then he realized there was no need. She was long dead, and any scent that might attract wolves or coyotes was long gone. He marveled that they hadn't attacked the grave earlier since they could smell a dead body under less than six feet of dirt. Maggie had been put in a two-foot-deep grave.

When he finished, he looked at Claudia, who held the silver locket up, letting it flash slowly in the sun as it rotated back and forth on its delicate chain.

"I'll give you a few minutes," Slocum said. "Then we had better get out of here."

"There's no gold," Claudia said sadly. "And my sister is dead. I didn't know. I didn't even suspect."

Slocum started to ask the questions that he wanted answered most, but turned away to leave Claudia with her grief for a few minutes. He worried about Neale and his gang showing up. He left the small grove and looked around, seeing other groupings of trees that could have been interpreted as being where the treasure was. As he walked around this part of the meadow slowly, he took in the terrain and the trees and knew they had been lucky—or unlucky—finding this particular spot where the woman had been buried.

He walked slowly back to the birch tree grove and saw Claudia wiping away tears. She stood and faced Slocum when she realized he was watching.

"Let's go. I . . . I want to paint some. As a tribute."

"You and your sister were close?"

"No," Claudia said, surprising Slocum yet again. "She was a terrible person. On any given day I might have called her a whore. In fact, more than once, I did." Claudia sniffed. "But she was blood kin, and that means something."

"You didn't know she was out here? Was she with your pa?"

"She might have seen him, but she wasn't *with* him," Claudia said positively. "He looked down on her loose ways. As any decent man would." Claudia glared at Slocum as if challenging him to contradict her. He said nothing.

"I want to paint," Claudia said.

"We have to leave," Slocum countered. "I told you why. The outlaws—"

"Won't bother us. Why should they? There's no gold, is there? Just a solitary, unmarked grave." Claudia chewed on her lower lip and came to a decision. "Perhaps later I'll mark her grave, but it doesn't seem right to do it now."

"They'll kill us," Slocum said. "They probably killed your sister. And your pa's nowhere to be seen, is he? They might have killed him too."

"I'll stay. You can go, John. You've been so kind to me."

Slocum didn't say another word. He turned, mounted, and rode off, but he found his path leading away from the northward trail to one going back into the canyon where Claudia had matched her painting with the mines on the slopes. He damned himself for being a fool, but he couldn't abandon Claudia to the outlaws, and he wasn't going to hogtie her and force her to accompany him. Either of those solutions rankled.

Slocum had to find the outlaws and figure out some way of decoying them away. A smile came to his lips. He wasn't above joining them, if they were going to make a quick raid on the Fort Union payroll. The smile faded when he realized that Neale wasn't likely to allow any newcomers to join his gang, especially one who looked like his mirror image. Slocum was better off trying to catch the leader of the road agents and turn him over to Marshal Hanks. And the chances of him accomplishing that were so small he couldn't begin to calculate them. Better to draw to an inside straight.

The meadow gave way to rockier terrain, and then he found the narrow trail going into the jaws of certain danger. Out of sight but not that far ahead, Slocum heard the clop-clop of several horses. The loud conversation among the men warned Slocum that he was going to locate the outlaws a lot easier than he had expected. They were riding the trail directly into the meadow—the one he was on.

Slocum realized how foolish this sally of his had been. Neal and his cutthroats weren't likely to accept him or let him ambush them one by one. Killing Neale might give him a little head start, but the way the outlaws had fought without their leader told him they were more likely to avenge Neale's death than run from the man causing it.

He wheeled his horse about and trotted back to warn Claudia. He hoped he was far enough ahead of the outlaws so the sounds of his passage wouldn't alert them. When he came to the widening in the trail, he put his heels to his horse's flanks and galloped back to the birch grove. His heart jumped into his throat when he saw the buckboard was gone—and so was the woman.

He stood in the stirrups and looked around, frantic to find her before the outlaws spilled into the meadow. He doubted Neale or any of the men with him would miss the fresh tracks made both by Slocum's horse and Claudia's buckboard. Where was she?

She'd said she wanted to find a spot to paint. Slocum couldn't understand the goad that drove her to such crazy behavior when running was obviously the way to stay alive and not end up in a shallow grave like Maggie. He didn't see her. He took a chance and called out to her.

"Claudia!" he shouted. No answer. Slocum dared not shout a second time or he would warn Neale of his location. He dismounted and studied the tracks in the grass left by the buckboard. He let out a gusty sigh of relief. She had driven toward another canyon. Slocum saw no sign that anyone else had joined her or coerced the woman to drive off. From the depth of the tracks, she had driven off alone in the buckboard.

Slocum swung into the saddle and trotted after her, hoping to be out of sight of the outlaws and into the canyon before they knew he even existed. Claudia might be safer if she had chosen some other canyon to explore, but Slocum doubted it. Neale and his gang roamed the entire region, either on patrol against lawmen or to find and rob careless travelers. Slocum wondered if the bounty hunter had provided enough distraction for Neale that the outlaw would be cautious when he rode into the meadow.

Still, the rocky canyon afforded little in the way of grass for their horses or water, while the meadow was a paradise. This convinced Slocum that Neale would spend some time in the meadow to rest his horses and men. He just hoped that Wilmer had done more than die fast under the outlaws' guns.

The buckboard trail led directly into a canyon branching off to the southwest. The sun was slanting down into his eyes, making it more difficult to ride and causing his shadow to stretch out behind him. Slocum worried that he would be easily seen from behind, outlined by the sun and unable to scramble to safety.

After ten minutes of riding, he felt he had gone far enough into the sheer-walled canyon to slow and give his horse a rest. He wished he had watered the horse before leaving Claudia the way he had. The horse was his only salvation, and if he ended up on foot again, he was a goner. When the horse began to stumble on the increasingly steep road, Slocum dismounted and walked. He reached the summit, out of breath and looking around in the hope of finding Claudia before the sun vanished behind the high mountain peaks. The road ahead wound back and forth and yielded no sign of the woman or her buckboard.

Slocum slogged downhill and for close to a mile before mounting again. Even then, his horse tried to rear. It wasn't up to carrying a man on its back, but Slocum gave it no choice. It took the better part of five minutes to calm the horse enough so he could ride on. He cursed the delay, but it was necessary if he wanted to keep his horse strong enough and peaceable enough to carry him. He regretted the death of the Appaloosa. That horse had possessed more heart than any other Slocum had owned in the past couple years.

He broke off his self-pity at losing such a magnificent horse when he saw a nearly blank canvas beside the road. Bending low without getting off the horse, Slocum snared the canvas and lifted it into the sunlight where he could look at it. Claudia had barely sketched on it. A few faint, tentative lines in the charcoal she used to rough in her subject might have represented the ridgeline of the mountains ahead, although Slocum couldn't tell. The picture was too incomplete.

"You can't be that much ahead of me," he said. Slocum urged his horse onward into the gathering twilight. All the time he kept one ear straining for the sound of pursuit. Only the steady sound of his own horse's hooves reached him in the gathering quiet as sunlight fled before the chilly night. He repressed the urge to call out to the woman again. Such a shout would echo back all the way to the meadow, bouncing off the almost vertical walls close by on either side.

The trail widened a mite, probably blasted into the side of the canyon wall to freight out ore from mines deeper in. The steepness caused Slocum to get off and walk again, but he saw occasional traces that the buckboard had come by recently. Claudia's team proved stronger than the stolen horse Slocum rode. And then he wasn't so sure he had come out with the low card in the deck.

Part of the roadway had collapsed recently and fallen into the ravine below. Slocum hurried upward now, his stride long and sure as fear for the woman drove him. He reached the top of the grade and saw where most of the road had broken free. Going to the edge of the sundered trail, he looked down into the shadowy ravine below.

All he saw was a rear wheel on the buckboard, slowly spinning. Of Claudia Peterson he saw no trace.

11

"Claudia!" Slocum dismounted and peered over the edge of the precipice. The distance wasn't as far as he feared, but the buckboard was pretty well destroyed. He looked for any sign of movement, and all he saw was the slowly turning wheel. "Claudia!"

He started down the side of the mountain, and then heard a sound that sent a cold chill up his spine.

"I tell you, Neale, I heard something."

"I did too," piped up another voice. A low murmur of several others told Slocum that Neale's entire gang was coming up the road behind him. He had only minutes before they came to the ruined stretch of road and saw Claudia's wagon below. For her to have any chance of surviving, Slocum had to do something. Fast.

He swung into the saddle and rode back along the road he had just traversed, his mind spinning through dozens of improbable ploys. He reached down, pulled his rifle from the scabbard, and levered in a round, then waited for the response he knew had to come.

Two riders crested the hill ahead of him. For a moment they were silhouetted against the evening sky. Slocum got off three shots, hitting one of the outlaws before both

ducked back. The loud cries of anger and rage convinced
Slocum he had gotten their attention. He urged his horse
through the rocks above the road. The way proved more
difficult than he had anticipated, and he was hardly off the
trail when four outlaws came galloping over the hill, six-
shooters blazing.

They had no idea where Slocum was and their lead ric-
ocheted off rocks all around. Slocum got off another shot
and hit one rider's horse. It went down and caused a mo-
mentary jumble in the road.

"Up the slope. Uphill. There's the son of a bitch!"

Slocum fired again, aware that the road agents were staring in his direction and the foot-long orange tongue of
flame from his rifle's muzzle would give him away. It
didn't matter. He had to decoy the gang away from Claudia.

He fired until the rifle came up empty. But the few
rounds were enough to drive the men to cover, allowing
Slocum breathing room. He kept his horse moving, got to
a large boulder, and put it between him and his would-be
killers. From here, Slocum caught a break. A game trail
wended its way higher. Slocum followed it, grateful that
he didn't have to pioneer a new trail through the darkness. All it took was for his horse to step on a Spanish
bayonet and have the plant's vicious spine driven into an
exposed leg. He kept moving, even after the horse started
to balk.

As sudden as lightning, Slocum came out on top of a
ridge overlooking the meadow. He took a minute to reload
his rifle and cocked his head to the side, listening hard for
pursuit. The outlaws obliged him. He waited several more
minutes until they found the game trail and started uphill
after him. Again he emptied his rifle, spreading confusion
among them. He knew from the angry shouts that he'd only
scared them. He had wanted to wing or kill one or two
more.

Rather than make a stand here, he went down the far

side of the hill back into the meadow. He gave the horse its head, letting it race for cover. He eventually found the stream cutting through the meadow and permitted his horse to drink. He took the opportunity to splash water on his own face, reload, and try to remember a spot in the meadow where a single man—him—would be at an advantage over a gang of owlhoots.

Slocum couldn't think of a single place in the wide-open, rolling meadow. He could find a hiding place and hope that Neale's men missed him, but that defeated his purpose of luring them away from Claudia if they returned to the canyon. Thought of the woman lying hurt, possibly unconscious, needing help at the bottom of the ravine, told him he had no choice. He had to keep the outlaws in the saddle and after him.

When his horse had drunk its fill and rested a mite, Slocum went back into the open meadow to let the outlaws spot him. The darkness worked against him, but he had no problem finding them. Dark splotches rode in a long line across the sward. Slocum picked the moving shadow he thought was at the far end of their line and began firing. Three quick shots, one of them finding a target.

"Jesus!" cried the wounded outlaw. "He shot me in the leg! Get him, get him 'fore I bleed to death!"

Slocum knew the man couldn't have been badly hurt or he would have demanded that his partners tend him rather than go after Slocum. That was fine. Slocum stayed still, waiting them out. When they didn't turn toward him, he felt secure in taking another shot into the night. This time one of the men spotted his muzzle flash.

Their long line swung around with the ease of long practice, and they caught Slocum in a semicircle, blocking him off from any of the canyons where he might hide. He was caught out in the open meadow. He wheeled his horse around and galloped for a stand of trees. The outlaws came after him like a machine, no one in the line getting ahead of the others. Slocum had thought he was up against a wild band of road agents, but Neale had trained them to military precision in their attacks.

Slocum was sorry now that he hadn't forced Claudia to leave when he'd had the chance. Neither of them might leave the Sangre de Cristo Mountains alive.

He ducked as he rode into a stand of pine trees. The forest got thicker ahead so Slocum veered to his left, thinking he might use the cover of the forest to outflank Neale's gang. He slowed to a walk and then halted to listen. The outlaws swept into the forest behind him. He edged away until the last of the trees was behind him. He could go straight for the canyon where Claudia had taken the plunge over the edge of the cliff, but he hesitated.

That saved his life.

Neale had left two men in the meadow to cover any such escape on his part. Slocum opened fire on them at the same instant they spotted him. In the dark their accuracy was poor, but so was his. Slocum realized he had more to lose than they did by keeping up the shooting. The gunfire pulled the rest of the gang out of the forest, back to the meadow, until he was outnumbered again.

"We don't want to kill you, mister! We want to know why you're shootin' at us!"

"That you, Neale?" Slocum took a chance using the outlaw's name. He wanted to keep the leader of the gang as confused as possible.

"You know me? That means you must be a lawman. You work for that jackass Leroy Hanks?"

"He's after me too."

"Then you must want to join me. Stop shooting, come out where we can see you, and let's palaver."

Slocum knew better. The riders with Neale were still moving to cut him off. If he fell into their trap, he would be dead before his feet hit the ground.

Slocum cursed under his breath. He had hoped to sneak

past the outlaws and return to help Claudia, but now keeping his own hide intact mattered more. He turned away from the men and rode back toward the forest. If he could reach the shelter of the trees, he might not evade Neale's gang, but he could give them a run for their money.

"He's gettin' away, Boss!"

"Charge!" Neale's command was as crisp and determined as any cavalry officer's. The thunder of hooves told Slocum that he had only a few seconds. He galloped for the woods and reached the edge. More and more low-hanging tree limbs raked at his face. He bent double, slowed, and rode at an angle intended to take him back toward the line of outlaws. If he had tried to go away, they would overtake him. He had to outflank them.

The trees continued to tear at his face and body, but Slocum pressed on until he thought he had ridden past the line of road agents. He turned back toward the meadow and once more came to the edge of the forest.

The outlaws had missed him. He was past them, but they were also between him and the mouth of the canyon he had to enter to help Claudia. Slocum rested, fuming at the inactivity but knowing he had no choice. Patience had always paid off for him when he was a sniper during the war, and it did now also. The outlaws hunted, and eventually reported to their leader that they had lost him. Slocum waited to see what Neale would do. He might send his men back in another sweep, forcing Slocum to move ahead like a cork bobbing on a pond, but Neale ordered his men to regroup.

Slocum saw the dark knot of outlaws, but could not overhear Neale's orders. Then his heart sank. The gang turned and rode back for the canyon they had just left. They would find Claudia, and there was nothing Slocum could do about it.

Following would be foolhardy, but Slocum had to be close if they found Claudia alive. He considered his chances and Claudia's, and then knew he could do nothing to save her right away. Let Neale and his gang find her. They wouldn't kill her outright. She was too beautiful a woman. Slocum knew he was condemning her to a terrible fate, but it might be worse getting them both killed by doing something dumb. Slocum pitched his bedroll and tried to sleep. Thoughts of the woman and how she might be dead haunted him. Just before daybreak, he got his gear together and rode into the canyon after the outlaws, determined to shoot it out with them if he could wrest Claudia from their grip.

Slocum reached the spot where the buckboard had gone over the verge of the road and looked down at the wreckage. He saw no indication that Neale or anyone else had been down there. Had they ridden past in the darkness, not even noticing the way the road had collapsed? It was possible, but Slocum had to check for himself.

He rode a ways farther hunting for the outlaws. He saw numerous spoor left by their passage, but the gang was long gone on their way to wherever. They roved the mountains endlessly, whether looking for likely travelers to rob or simply to keep away from the lawmen like Marshal Hanks, Slocum couldn't say.

"Might be they're looking for something," Slocum said aloud. "Like the gold Claudia's pa stole."

He found a path down into the ravine and made his way lower until he reached the bottom and quickly rode to the wreckage. It looked worse from above than it did straight on, but Slocum didn't see any trace of the team—or Claudia. He poked around the buckboard and its scattered contents searching for blood. He found a smear, long since dried, on the seat. Other than this, there was no trace of Claudia or any indication how badly she'd been hurt by the tumble down the slope.

Slocum walked in ever-widening circles around the buckboard, but couldn't find her tracks. The entire area was mostly rock with little vegetation. And what did grow here forced its way up through stone crevices. Some distance from the buckboard he found the painting done by Claudia's father. Slocum lifted it high to see how badly damaged it had been. To his surprise, it was almost intact. Deep scratches across the top were the only damage. Slocum carried it back to the buckboard and leaned it against a wheel. Stepping back, he stared hard at the painting, as if he knew something about art and the skill it took to paint such a piece.

In spite of his lack of appreciation for such things, he felt some emotional connection with it the longer he stared. Claudia's pa had been a good painter and had captured the scenery well. What more had he captured and put into that painting? Slocum hunkered down and studied the cigar-shaped section at the bottom where Claudia had pressed the paintbrush she'd found at the bottom of the mine shaft.

Slocum stood and began hunting for the paintbrush. It took him almost twenty minutes to find where it had been flung when the buckboard tipped over onto its side. He returned to the painting, put the brush handle into place on the bottom, and thought a while on both the small arrow inscribed on the wood handle and what it might mean. He was experienced at reading maps, but it didn't make much sense to him that the arrow pointed in the direction of the treasure.

"North is usually at the top of a map," he said, turning the painting so that the brush pointed upward. Slocum almost dropped the painting when he saw words appear. He tipped the painting back, and they disappeared unless he canted his head to one side. The artist had disguised the word "here" amid the mines and rock tailings he had drawn.

Slocum studied the painting more carefully, and saw a faint dotted line pointing to one of the deserted mines in the canyon where the artwork had been made.

"Didn't have to come this way at all. Or go back to the meadow," Slocum said. He wondered at the cruel fate that had led Claudia to her sister's grave the way it had. There wasn't anything in the painting that should have led her to the grave, yet it had.

Just as the painting was going to take Slocum to the gold.

Slocum repacked the painting in its crate and slung it on the back of his horse. Then he made one last circuit of the area to find any tracks Claudia might have left. If she had bled in the wagon, then she must have left a bloody trail. But try as he might, Slocum couldn't find any direction where Claudia might have gone. Either up or down the ravine seemed likely, but she might also have headed for the far wall of the canyon, thinking to get away from the road and the wreckage, should someone like Neale and his gang come looking for her.

Slocum considered shouting her name again, but didn't know how far off the outlaws might be. After the merry chase he had led them on the night before, they would gleefully fill him full of holes if they came within range.

Giving up his hunt, Slocum took what supplies he could from the buckboard, and then made his way back up the gravelly slope to the trail and finally out of the canyon into the meadow. He heaved a sigh of relief getting away from the outlaws. Or so he hoped. At least he wasn't caught on a narrow track where he couldn't dodge.

Until he went back into the canyon where the landscape had been painted. The difference this time would be the promise of gold.

Slocum pondered on taking the gold and not finding Claudia. It was her gold, after all. A slow smile came to his lips. It wasn't her gold, though. Or her pa's. It had been stolen, probably from the Army. That didn't bother him in the least. He could pack up the gold and hightail it north into Colorado before anyone knew.

Slocum rode a little straighter as he hit the trail, and felt much happier at the notion he was going to be paid so handsomely for being chased by lawmen and gunmen and probably lied to by a very lovely woman.

He was going to be rich.

12

The terrain between the road and the mines on the far side of the canyon was too rugged for Slocum to ride over, but he tried. As his horse gingerly picked its way through the fist-sized rocks littering the way, he realized he wasn't going to make it all the way without the horse breaking a leg. Reluctantly, Slocum dismounted and took the painting from its crate. He placed it against a rock, pressed the brush into place, and turned the canvas to orient it as if the arrow pointed north. Again he made out wavy lettering saying "here" and a dotted line wandering around the hillside up to a mine.

"That's the one," Slocum said to himself. Then he frowned. He might be reading something more into the painting than was there. The lettering looked obvious enough when the painting was tilted at the proper angle, but it might be coincidence. He had spent too much time in saloons staring into beer mugs, watching bubbles form faces and other recognizable patterns on the surface. Turning the painting another quarter turn caused the lettering to disappear, but other possibilities presented themselves. Had Claudia's father put them in to confuse anyone looking at the painting without the paintbrush? Or was Slocum imagining it all?

The more he thought, the less sure he was that any gold lay at the end of this trail.

"Come this far, might as well go the rest of the way," he told the horse. He patted the animal's neck. A big brown eye glared at him. Slocum didn't put much store in any animal's thinking ability, but this one resented him. The way the horse glared whenever he tried to gentle it told him he ought to get rid of the horse, first chance, and find a new mount.

"I'll just hobble you here and go take a look," Slocum said. As he worked to place the hobbles on the horse's front legs, he looked up the slope to the mine and its tailings. Getting there might take the better part of a day. Slocum stuffed an extra box of ammo in his coat pocket, shook his canteen and was pleased to find that it was full, then started up the rocky hillside.

After twenty minutes of slipping and sliding, he began to wonder how the miners had ever gotten to their claim, much less an artist lugging a load of stolen gold. As Slocum rested, he looked around for a trail up to the mine, even one overgrown with weeds or covered by rock slides. He wasn't sure he found it, but began edging along the mountainside to get to a faint line against the rock.

He found the trail and guessed that it hadn't been used much in the past several years. Slocum had no idea when all the mines had played out, or if the miners had simply given up because they hadn't found any pay dirt. He trooped up the trail, panting for breath within minutes. The altitude got to him, and he hadn't taken time for a decent meal. He realized the gold fever had infected him and made it hard for him to think straight. He should never have run off leaving Claudia—or her body—in the other canyon. That was more of a crime to him than shooting any of the outlaws in the back from ambush.

Taking a long swig of tepid water from his canteen, he

looked up and gauged the distance to the mine. It might take another hour. He wished he had a burro, as the miner who had dug that hole must have had. Slinging the canteen again, he had begun to hike when he heard a rasping sound that froze him in his tracks.

His hand flashed to his six-shooter. He drew, spun, and aimed, only to lower the hammer when he saw the source of the heavy breathing.

"Never thought I'd come across you again," he said to the bounty hunter. Wilmer lay sprawled below a towering rock above the trail. Through force of will, he had crawled far enough up to be able to see Slocum.

"You gotta help me. Gotta. I'm gonna die if 'n you don't."

"You'd've dragged me back to Las Vegas for the reward. You're sure I'm not Neale, aren't you?"

"No-account bastard shot me. He laughed as he shot me. Ran outta ammo and had my hands in the air. He shot me fer no reason."

"He had plenty of reason," Slocum said, edging up through the jumble of rocks to reach the bounty hunter. "He didn't want you dogging his tracks like you'd done to me."

"You ain't an outlaw, are you?"

"My name's Slocum, and I'd never heard of Neale until the Las Vegas marshal threw me in jail and you came after me outside Taos. I think the station agent in Las Vegas mistook me for the outlaw. He was mighty nearsighted and I do look more than a passing amount like Neale."

"Sorry 'bout the confusion. You gotta help me or I'll die."

Slocum clambered to the top of the boulder and saw that Wilmer was in a bad way. He had been shot more than once in the belly. A pang of memory stabbed into Slocum's soul. He had objected to the way William Quantrill had killed every male over the age of eight in Lawrence, Kansas. For his concern, he had been shot in the belly by Bloody Bill Anderson and left to die. But he had been too ornery for that. It had taken months of pain and determination to recover. Slocum wasn't about to leave anybody to die who had been similarly shot.

"There's not a hell of a lot I can do for you," Slocum said, tearing away the bounty hunter's buckskin shirt. He probed the wounds and saw they were bad, but not as bad as all the blood suggested. Wilmer would still die unless he got to a doctor.

"Git me to Taos. There's a *curandero* there what kin fix me up."

"Better than a doctor could," Slocum allowed. Some healing herbs made into a poultice might heal the wounds better than a doctor poking around with a wire probe and a blunt knife. From the entry and exit wounds, Wilmer had been as lucky as he could be. The slugs had gone clean through him. That left behind a powerful lot of damage inside, but Wilmer had been coping with that all right up till now.

"Here's some water," Slocum said, passing over his canteen. He sliced up the bloody buckskin and made a crude bandage from it. The wounds wouldn't bleed if pressure was kept on them. But moving Wilmer might open them. If he started bleeding, he was a goner.

"Much obliged."

"You still have a horse?"

"Gone," Wilmer said. "Reckon Neale stole it. Wouldn't put it past him to steal a man's horse. He's stole 'bout everything else."

"What's got the law so riled? Neale's a real owlhoot, but not the worst I ever heard. Why's Marshal Hanks so hot to track him down?"

Wilmer looked at Slocum, his lips quivering from weakness. He finally formed the words.

"Same reason I want him."

"More than the hundred-dollar reward," Slocum said. "You want the gold. Where'd Neale get it?"

"He's a cashiered Army captain. They caught 'im cheatin' in the quartermaster's accounts."

"Taking his own cut off the payroll?"

"Don't know. Prob'ly," grunted Wilmer as Slocum cinched up the bandages. "He lit out 'fore the court-martial. Figger he was the one what robbed the stagecoach of the Fort Union payroll. Him and some of his men that deserted along with 'im."

"So the Army wants him as bad as the law."

"Been cuttin' quite a swath through the countryside since he deserted," Wilmer said. "The Army didn't identify him till last week or two."

"That's why Marshal Hanks didn't clap me in jail the first time he laid eyes on me," Slocum said. "I must have been lucky since he got the news about Neale from the station agent, who must have been alerted by his home office. I was fool enough to ride back in on my way north."

Wilmer stared hard at Slocum. "Why'd you go back to Las Vegas?"

"Let's say a business opportunity I was looking into didn't pan out."

"You was thinkin' on holdin' up the stage, weren't you?"

"I can let you rot on this rock. There're plenty of buzzards circling overhead," Slocum said.

"You didn't commit no crime I'm aware of," Wilmer said pragmatically. "Even if you did, what reward would be out on a skinny feller like you wouldn't be anywhere near what my life's worth."

"You think you can make it all the way back?"

"Can't ask you to go to Las Vegas," Wilmer said. "Besides, I think Taos is closer by a day's travel."

"You know these hills better than I do. How do we get there in a hurry?"

"You need your horse. Hell, *I* need your horse. Walkin' ain't gonna work for me, not after I get down this hill."

"Let's get moving," Slocum said, casting a look back up

the hill to the mine. Was the gold there? He wouldn't know until after he got Wilmer settled in Taos.

"Come on," Slocum said. He got his arm around the much shorter man's shoulders and lifted. Slocum staggered under the added weight. Wilmer was heavier than he looked.

Slocum round it easier following the trail down now that he was on it. From the direction, it would come out in the ravine a quarter mile or so farther north of where he'd left his horse. There wasn't any way around this, not with Wilmer's condition.

When Slocum felt the bounty hunter begin to fade away, he asked, "How'd Neale come to lose the gold?"

"Who says he lost it?"

"He's prowling these mountains like a caged cougar," Slocum said. "That tells me he's looking for something."

"A woman, that's how he lost it. Ain't it always the way?"

"Maggie Peterson?"

"Don't know her name, but she's cute as a button, from accounts."

"I found a grave in the meadow. Think Neale killed her?"

"Never heard that. Heard she stole the gold from him and that's enough to make a man like him kill his own mother. She musta hid it somewhere around here."

They stumbled and staggered along until they reached the ravine.

Wilmer said, "I gotta rest. Took a powerful lot outta me, gettin' up there and comin' back."

"How'd you get away from Neale?"

"He gut-shot me and rolled me down into the arroyo. Took my horse. But I figgered he might come back to be sure I was dead, so I thought gettin' over the hill'd hide me away from him."

Slocum looked back up the steep hill and remembered how hard it had been for him to make it. He touched his own wounds, but they hardly gave a twinge. He couldn't imagine the determination it had taken on Wilmer's part to get as far as he had.

"How much?" Slocum asked.

"What?"

"How much gold did Neale steal?"

"Payroll's usually more 'n a thousand dollars."

"That's damned near five pounds of gold," Slocum said.

"Gold coins," Wilmer agreed. "Easy to spend, nobody'd question you 'bout it if you gave 'em a twenty-dollar gold piece. Quite a reward fer gettin' shot in the gut."

"Or getting a gut-shot man to a doctor," Slocum said, smiling. "You stay here now and don't go running off. I'll fetch my horse."

"Jist 'cuz you're so purty, I'll wait around fer you," Wilmer said, grimacing as he sank to the ground. "Don't be too long or I might not have a choice."

Slocum retrieved his horse and got them on the trail to Taos just before sundown.

Wilmer had been unconscious for the last day. Slocum had stopped frequently to dribble water into the man's mouth, and had been reassured that the bounty hunter was still alive by the weak response. But Slocum faced another problem as he walked slowly toward the trading town. The town marshal wasn't likely to be too inclined toward him, but the real worry came from Marshal Hanks. The Las Vegas lawman had the smell of gold in his nose, and wasn't likely to give up on it, any more than a bloodhound quit following a scent.

He heaved a sigh and kept walking. Wilmer was going to die if Slocum didn't find him help soon.

"No doctor," Wilmer gasped out. "Don't cotton to 'em. Gimme a *curandero.*"

"I ought to get you a *bruja*," Slocum said.

"Better 'n any doctor. Always usin' them sharp knives of theirs when they don't have to."

Wilmer passed out again.

Slocum wondered if he might come to life when they passed an adobe with a painted sign proclaiming it to be the surgery of the town doctor. Considering the man's antipathy toward doctors, Slocum was inclined to pass on by, but a young man stepped out into the bright noonday sun and rolled down his sleeves.

"You!" he called. "You there, the one with the man slung over the saddle. He's hurt. Where are you going?"

"He wants a *curandero*," Slocum said, not adding that Wilmer would cheerfully slit the throat of a doctor before letting one cut on him.

"He's lost a powerful lot of blood," the young doctor said, going to Wilmer and lifting his head using a handful of hair. "What happened?"

"Two shots to the belly. Close up. Both slugs went clean through him."

"How long ago?"

"Three days," Slocum said. "Been taking it slow getting here because he's so weak."

"You should have sent someone to fetch me."

"There's just me and him," Slocum said. "Didn't think it was a good idea to leave him out in the mountains alone."

The doctor cast a sharp look at Slocum, then nodded once.

"Get him inside. I'll see what has to be done."

"Might be a *curandero* can help?"

"He has the look of a mountain man about him." The doctor wrinkled his nose at the smell rising off Wilmer. "I've dealt with his kind before. What about you?"

"Do you mean, am I going to fight you over this? You think you'd stand much chance if I did?"

"No, but I'd try."

"If you're that determined to get a patient, you'll be that determined to save him," Slocum said, sliding Wilmer off the saddle and getting him over one shoulder. He staggered a little under the bounty hunter's weight as he went into the surgery. The place smelled of carbolic acid and made Slocum's nose wrinkle. But it was a smell he knew well from the war. It was better than the rotting-meat odor that permeated some doctors' offices.

"Over there," ordered the doctor, pouring carbolic acid over his hands and then putting on a bleached white coat. He waited impatiently as Slocum positioned Wilmer on a table and stepped away. The doctor crowded past and began using a sharp knife on the bounty hunter's clothing to cut it away from his wounds. All the while he muttered to himself.

"What do you want me to do?" Slocum asked.

"You got any gunshots that need tending?"

Slocum touched his side and then shook his head.

"Then go on down the street and get Señora Vargas. Tell her to bring two of her special poultices. She'll know what I want."

"You on good terms with her?"

The doctor smiled wanly, then said, "I thought I knew it all till I saw how she used those herbs and nettles and other less mentionable things to help people. Whatever she puts into her wound poultice is better than anything I can do. This man's lost a considerable amount of blood, and the poultice will help stop more bleeding. Now git!"

Slocum got. He stepped back into the hot afternoon sun and stretched his muscles. On the lookout for the Taos marshal or Leroy Hanks, Slocum found Señora Vargas and told her what was needed.

"So, Dr. Lennox needs me again?"

"Looks like," Slocum said. His nose wrinkled when he caught the scent rising from the pot on the stove. Unlike carbolic acid, this was stomach-turning. It didn't surprise him when she ladled out a full tin pot of the gunk, put a lid on it, and handed it to Slocum.

"Take this to the doctor. He knows how to use it. I have shown him."

"Much obliged. What do I owe you?"

The woman waved him off, saying, "I need nothing but the doctor's admission I know more than he does."

Slocum made his way back to the doctor's office, and got inside in time to see Lennox cleaning the last of the blood off Wilmer's hide.

"Just in time. Smear some of that paste on either side, and I'll bandage him up."

Slocum slathered the milky-white glue where the doctor pointed. Wilmer stirred and made a sound like a coyote pup. He stirred as the doctor tightened the bandages, and then looked up accusingly at Slocum.

"I tole you what I'd do, Slocum. I warn't foolin'."

"The *curandera* just left," the doctor said. "She told me to bandage you up for her. Since Señora Vargas doesn't have room for you, you'll have to stay here. Maybe a day, but no longer. I need the table for my poker game."

Slocum appreciated the way Lennox spoke firmly, giving Wilmer the information he wanted to hear, yet telling the bounty hunter what was going to happen—no argument allowed.

"Git on out of here, Doc," the bounty hunter said.

"Might as well. You're not going to die, so I can get myself a drink. Otherwise, I'd be wasting my time and could go fetch the undertaker. He's a regular son of a bitch when it comes to indigents."

Slocum sidled away as the doctor grabbed his coat to leave them alone for a spell. He fumbled around in his vest and came out with the twenty-dollar gold piece and handed it to Lennox.

"This'll buy me more than a bottle of whiskey," the doctor said. "I'll let the cantina give me enough change to pay Señora Vargas and whatever I decide it's worth putting up with a cantankerous galoot like him. You ought to get back ten-twelve dollars."

"Much obliged," Slocum said.

The doctor flipped the tiny coin in the air, catching it deftly.

"No, I'm much obliged. I thought I'd be stuck with trying to sell his buckskin shirt as rags to get my fee." Lennox left, whistling tunelessly.

Slocum glanced at the discarded buckskin and shook his head. There were hardly bloody tatters left. The doctor was quite a joker.

"Slocum," rasped out Wilmer. "We gotta talk, you 'n me."

"What do you need? Water?"

"A partner. I ain't never said this to no one before, but I think me and you ought to team up. There's a powerful lot of them outlaws in Neale's gang fer one man to tackle."

"But the pair of us would be up to the chore?"

"More 'n up to it. Them varmints will turn tail and run jist hearin' we're after 'em."

Slocum chuckled at this arrogance. Then he considered how hard it would be getting back into the middle of the Sangre de Cristo Mountains to find the gold. Neale was a cold-blooded killer. Wilmer was testament to that, as was Maggie Peterson in her lonely grave. For all he knew, Neale had also caught Claudia by now and killed her.

He might get back and find the gold hidden in the mine—or it might not be there at all. Slocum considered whether it was better to split the take, if it even existed, and have Wilmer guarding his back, or to go back into the mountains alone.

"Partners," Slocum said, thrusting out his hand. Wilmer took it in a surprisingly strong grip.

"Partners."

Slocum wondered what the hell he had just gotten himself into.

13

"Cain't git over how friendly that there doctor was," Wilmer said. "He fixed me up real good, though he did know to go to the *curandera* when it came to real medicine." Wilmer scratched his ribs and twisted from side to side, testing the limits of motion. "Feel better, but not up to snuff. Not all the way."

"You did all right getting a horse as fast as you did. How'd you pay for it?" Slocum looked ahead down the pass leading into the meadow, which would be their last stop before hunting for the mine where he thought the gold was hidden.

"Knew people," Wilmer said vaguely. "People willin' to give me a horse in exchange."

"In exchange for what?"

"Not turnin' them over to the law. The rewards on their heads didn't amount to a hill o' beans, but they didn't know that. They figgered a horse in exchange fer me fergettin' where they are was just peachy."

Slocum wondered if there had been more to the transaction, but the Taos marshal wasn't galloping down on them, waving a noose around in the air and screaming that they were horse thieves. He was willing to believe Wilmer. A little.

"Real purty country," Wilmer said, pausing to study the meadowlands as they came to the top of the pass leading down into the grassy area. "A man could do worse than have a spread here."

"I'm more interested in the gold," Slocum said. "What do you know of Maggie Peterson's pa?"

"Cain't say I know much of anything 'bout him. She was in with Neale, but I heard tell she had a partner. Could be it was her pa."

"I haven't seen hide nor hair of anyone other than Neale and his gang—and you—since coming to this part of the world," Slocum said, thinking on the matter a bit harder. How could a man let Neale kill his daughter and not be outraged? It was possible Neale had dispatched Peterson just after he sent the painting to Claudia. Had Neale known the painting was a map to where the gold was hidden—and who had hidden the stolen cavalry payroll?

Slocum looked sideways at his new partner. Wilmer had recovered in less than a week and hardly showed the effects of being drilled twice in the belly.

He was a potent force of nature.

"You pick that hill where I found you for any particular reason?" Slocum asked.

"Naw, I was only pawin' my way up to get to the top of the hill. If I'd got that far, I could lose Neale fer good." Wilmer turned in the saddle and stared at Slocum. "You figger that there hill's where the gold is hid?"

"I do. The painting Claudia Peterson had was a map made by her pa, but it had information hidden away in it. I think I found part of it, but I need to look at the painting again to be certain."

"Don't matter. If the gold's in one of them mines, there's no way we can miss findin' it. There's only a handful—"

"Three."

"Three of them there mines. We kin find the gold if we

look long enough. We're gonna be rich, Slocum. Richer than if I'd turned you over to Marshal Hanks fer the reward."

"Why's the reward so low on Neale? A hundred dollars hardly seems enough for someone who's stolen a thousand-dollar payroll."

"They were offerin' more alive than dead. I bet the Army wanted to sweat it out of him where he hid the money. They was settin' on the wanted poster fer a long time, their own patrols out huntin' fer the varmint. When they couldn't find 'im, they musta put out the reward."

"How'd you get on the trail so fast?"

"I was hangin' 'round the post, that's how. You never kin tell what'll turn up at Fort Union. Big post. Huge. Lots of supplies goin' in and out all the time."

Slocum read more into the bounty hunter's words, than Wilmer actually said. Wilmer wasn't above doing a little stealing of his own. If he had a chance, he would have stolen the payroll himself. Since the cavalry was so stirred up over Neale and the theft, he'd had no chance to do anything like it on his own. Slocum guessed Wilmer had been living off the post garbage when the commanding officer had finally let the station agent in Las Vegas know they wanted a former officer for desertion and robbery.

They rode down into the meadow. Slocum stared at the birch grove where Claudia's sister was buried and wondered if her father was also nearby, a feast for the maggots.

"That the right canyon?" Wilmer pointed.

"You don't know?" A dozen wild thoughts raced through Slocum's head. If Wilmer didn't know where he had been shot, he didn't know where the three mines on the steep hillside were either. Even as the thought of double-crossing Wilmer crossed his mind, Slocum pushed it away. They were partners, and partners didn't cheat each other. The bounty hunter would be useful in reaching the hidden gold and in getting it out of the mountains. They could split the take and go their separate ways then, and Slocum wouldn't have the burden of watching Wilmer's back—or the relief of having the bounty hunter watching his.

"Cain't say I do," replied Wilmer. "I spent most o' my time with my nose to the ground trackin' folks. Didn't matter to me where I was as much as who I was huntin'."

Slocum had the uneasy feeling Wilmer was lying through his broken, blackened teeth. He was on old mountain man and never forgot a single landmark, a single stone or turn of river or canyon. In that shaggy head must reside a virtual map of every inch of these mountains.

"It's where Claudia Peterson ran off the road," Slocum said. "We find the spot where the road collapsed under her buckboard, then we find the painting and get on up to the mines."

"But you don't know which one's hidin' the gold?"

Slocum shook his head. He rode slowly, alert for any sign of Neale or his gang. More than the road agents, Slocum was hunting for Claudia. It still bothered him that he hadn't found her body at the bottom of the slope amid the wreckage.

"There's the break in the road," Wilmer said. He didn't try to contain his eagerness. "Downslope. Dang. I see it! There's the busted-up buckboard."

Slocum wished the bounty hunter wouldn't sound so cheerful. A woman had probably died down there. Then he frowned as the thought occurred to him that Neale had no reason to take her body, and there had not been evidence of a new grave anywhere. That meant Claudia was likely alive and Neale's prisoner.

Or had wolves dragged her body away? Slocum just couldn't tell.

"How do we git down there?" asked Wilmer. "The horses'll bust their fool legs tryin' to go straight down."

"Farther along the road is an easy way down; then we can double back along the ravine."

"Hell's bells, Slocum. Time's a-wastin'. I want to be rich!"

Wilmer edged along the narrow place in the road, then galloped off in search of the trail Slocum had taken earlier. Slocum followed more slowly, scanning the entire ravine from the elevated road for any trace of Claudia. He saw nothing by the time he reached the bottom of the slope.

"Where's that damn fool thing?" he heard Wilmer howl. The bounty hunter thrashed about like a bear with its foot in a trap. By the time Slocum reached the wrecked buckboard, Wilmer was red in the face and hammering his fist into the wood. "Where *is* it?"

"What's wrong?"

"That painting. The one you said showed where the gold was. I don't see it nowhere!"

"I left it a ways off," Slocum said. He rode across the gravel-bottomed ravine to the spot where he had begun the climb before finding Wilmer all shot up. Slocum frowned when he didn't find the painting where he had left it. He rode up and down the ravine for almost a hundred yards, in case he was wrong about the spot. He might not have the memory of a mountain man for terrain, but he couldn't have made a mistake of such proportions. The painting was gone.

He hopped to the ground and went to the rock where he had leaned the painting when he had studied it. Even the paintbrush was gone. He ran his fingers over the rock and came away with a blue smear.

"Somebody took it. Some paint rubbed off. This was where I left it." Slocum held up his fingers with the bright blue smear to show Wilmer.

"Neale! That thievin' son of a bitch done it to me again!"

Slocum sat on the rock and wiped the paint from his fingers. He felt suddenly tired. The painting had vanished.

Claudia was dead. The gold might or might not be up in one of the mines. He had succumbed to gold fever and lost his common sense, at least for a while.

"It's no good, Wilmer. We ought to get the hell out of here before Neale and his henchmen find us."

"I want the damned gold!" Wilmer roared. "He ain't gonna cheat me out of it. Not again."

"Again?" Slocum looked sharply at the bounty hunter.

"I mean, I had him before and he slipped through my fingers. He's a slippery bastard."

Slocum heard slyness rather than truth in the man's words, but shrugged it off. He meant it. Let Wilmer keep hunting for the gold and Neale. Colorado sounded better and better to Slocum.

"I'm moving on," Slocum said. "There's nothing for me here."

"The gold, man! The gold!"

"It's the Lost Dutchman Mine all over. I could have been entirely wrong about what I saw in the painting. And there may not be any gold. I paid for your doctor bills with a twenty-dollar gold piece I took off one of Neale's men. You said the payroll was in gold coins. Might be he divvied it up among his men and that was all that's left."

"You never tole me 'bout that," Wilmer said, glaring.

"Fact is, I didn't know about the payroll then, and it only just occurred to me. Like it's occurred to me I could be entirely wrong about the painting being a map."

"Then we gotta find it so you can be sure," Wilmer said. "I'm the best damn tracker anywhere in the Rocky Mountains." Wilmer dropped to his hands and knees like a dog and began sniffing around. Slocum sat and watched. The man did everything but bark and wag his tail when he found a trail.

"This way, Slocum. The owlhoot what took the map went this way."

"The painting," Slocum corrected, but he jumped down

from the rock to see what Wilmer had scouted out on the ground. It was a faint but definite partial footprint in a patch of soft dirt that Slocum should have found if he hadn't been so down in the mouth over all that had happened.

"Cain't tell how big the varmint makin' the print was. Not enough of it, but it's fresh. And he went thata way." Wilmer pointed back toward the buckboard.

Slocum walked alongside Wilmer as they went back to the wreckage. Here Slocum used his own considerable skill to hunt for any sign that Claudia had died. He only confirmed his earlier observation that there wasn't much blood if she had been seriously hurt. Still, she might have been thrown free as the buckboard tumbled down the hill and hit her head. He worked around the entire area and found no trace of blood.

"This way, Slocum. This way," Wilmer said, waving to him. He had gone a dozen paces up the ravine. "Found another footprint. Or piece of one. Somebody was tryin' to be careful, but I'm too good fer 'em."

Slocum and Wilmer made their way along the ravine until Slocum saw a rock dislodged on a slope leading up the side of the canyon. A quick look around showed that there were shallow caves above.

"Up there," Slocum said.

"No, no, Slocum, you got it all wrong. You must be blind as a bat. See this? He went on ahead."

Slocum didn't see anything. He looked back up to the shallow depressions in the side of the hill.

"Up there," he insisted.

"You go on, waste yer time. I'm goin' after that there painting." Wilmer strode off purposefully, now and then dropping to all fours to look for traces of the trail he followed. Or thought he followed.

Slocum took two quick steps, jumped up onto the rim of the arroyo, and quickly found a more distinct footprint. He had wondered about the size of the foot making the other tracks. There was no question who had put this one into the dirt.

Claudia Peterson had climbed up higher on the mountainside.

Slocum began trooping up the slope, aware of how weary he was from the trip to Taos and back with Wilmer. Telling the bounty hunter he would partner up with him seemed less important as he caught scent of cooking meat coming from a cave. He slipped the leather thong off his Colt Navy and then went into the smoke-filled cave.

"You'll choke yourself to death," he told Claudia. The woman jumped a foot. Her violet eyes went wide as she tried to speak, but nothing came out. "Mind if I help myself to a little bit of this?" Slocum sat down, waved his hand a few times to move the smoke away from his burning eyes, and then plucked at a piece of bacon Claudia had frying in the pan.

"How'd you find me?"

"I'm glad to see you too," he said. The bacon was half-raw, but tasted fine to him. He tried to remember the last time when he had eaten and couldn't. That was a sure sign he ought to chow down while he had the chance.

"I didn't mean it like that, John. You know that. I was trying to hide so they wouldn't find me."

"The outlaws?"

"They ride back and forth all the time. I have to be very careful when I venture out. I've only been going out at dusk and dawn, coming back here during the day and fearing for my life at night. There are animals out there!"

"Two- and four-legged," Slocum agreed. He tried a second piece of bacon, but the first had turned his stomach. Claudia hadn't scraped enough of the mold off it before frying it. "How'd you get away from the buckboard without a scratch?"

"I . . . I jumped at the right time, I suppose," Claudia said. She had a wild look about her that was slowly going away. Slocum had startled her more than he'd thought possible. "I landed in a patch of something stickery but wasn't hurt any."

"Lucky."

"I was *frightened,* John. I was sure the outlaws would catch me. I saw them ride by a couple times and they never spotted the buckboard, but I couldn't take a chance."

"Nope, of course not," Slocum said. He leaned back against the cave wall and saw the map painting behind Claudia. She tried to shift to hide it, and then saw he recognized it for what it was.

"I found it some distance from the wreck," she said.

"You saw me poking around and didn't think anyone would take the painting. When I went up the hillside, you grabbed the painting."

"You never came back, John."

He considered this and saw some truth in it. He had found Wilmer, and this had slowed him down when he returned, but he found it unlikely Claudia hadn't seen him.

"I reckon you did too good a job of hiding your footprints," Slocum said, "for me to track you. Have you found the gold?"

"No," she almost whined. "I've hunted everywhere, but there's so much around here. I don't even know what to do." She reached down and picked up the paintbrush. She jabbed it at him like a sword. "You knew what this meant. You lit out like you knew exactly where to go, but I looked everywhere and didn't find the gold."

"Your pa was clever the way he hid it," Slocum allowed. "I think there's writing on the painting."

"What? I never saw it!"

Slocum gestured for her to hand him the painting. He wasn't sure why he bothered, but being this close to Claudia again scrambled his common sense like a plate of eggs.

He edged toward the cave mouth and held up the painting out of the smoke to catch the light. Turning the painting, he said, "See this here?" He ran his finger along the word and dotted line. "I don't know where this goes, but it looks like it points to this mine."

"I looked there. I looked in all three of them," Claudia said. "But I appreciate you being honest with me, John." Claudia moved a little closer and Slocum felt the heat, not from the fire in the cave but from the woman's eyes. She laid her hand on his leg and moved it little by little to his crotch. She found the growing lump there and began massaging slowly.

"Don't start something you aren't willing to finish," Slocum said.

"I want to start," she said, her eyes closing. "And I want you to finish it." She moved even closer and let Slocum kiss her. All the while he was sampling the sweet, tender lips, her hand worked on him, making him uncomfortably hard in his jeans. Somehow, as they kissed, she managed to get a couple of fly buttons open. He popped out into her hand.

"So warm, so big, all mine," she whispered. Her feverish violet eyes looked into his green ones; then she dived down to the fleshy pillar she clutched so hard. Her lips kissed the very tip, and then opened enough to allow him to slide into the humid warmth of her mouth. A shudder passed through Slocum's body as he leaned back and let the eager woman tongue and kiss him.

He ran his hands through her hair, guiding her up and down at a pace that sent his pulse pounding like a smithy's hammer hitting an anvil. Every time her tongue flicked out and touched the sensitive underside, a new tremor passed through Slocum and caused him to get even harder. He saw her cheeks go hollow as she applied suction. This was almost more than he could take. He pulled her mouth away.

"My turn," he said.

"Your turn? What could you possibly do to excite me as much as I excite you?" she taunted. "Maybe you'll open my blouse and play with my breasts." She pulled open the now-dirty blouse and exposed the twin melons bobbing delightfully. Cupping them, she lifted first one and then the other, as if trying to take her own nipples into her mouth. "Or you could twist them a mite. Like this." Claudia's fingers caught the cherry-red nubs and turned from side to side until her breathing came in hard, sharp pants.

"You're getting all the pleasure, and there's nothing I'm doing. You've been alone too long," he said. He pulled her close, crushing her naked breasts against his chest as he kissed her lips. Moving from her lips, he covered her forehead and cheeks and closed eyes with kisses before moving lower. Her head tipped back. He kissed the hollow of her slender throat, and then slipped down between the fleshy mounds that captivated him so much.

Licking and sucking, he tended first one crest and then the other. He felt the nipples pulsing with every throb of the woman's heart. Pressing his tongue down hard, he buried the nip amid snowy white flesh and then released it suddenly. He repeated this on her other perfect breast, then suckled until moans of delight came from Claudia's lips.

Only then did he work lower. He wasn't as dexterous opening the buttons holding her skirt, but there was no hurry, in spite of the volcanic feelings mounting within his loins. He knew she enjoyed the slowness, the careful attention to her every bare section of flesh. He tongued and kissed and fondled and finally worked off her skirt.

She kicked free of the skirt, naked below the waist and with her blouse hanging open. He might have seen a prettier sight in his day, but he couldn't remember it now. She tossed her skirt behind her onto the cave floor and moved to lie on it. As she moved into position, Slocum stroked over her fine legs and cupped her buttocks, lifting them off the floor. Her legs parted wantonly for him.

"I want you, John. I want you so much!"

"What is it about me you want?" he teased.

"Everything. Everything! And this!" She made a wild grab between his legs and caught his pulsating column. She pulled him straight for her nether lips. When the purpled head of his manhood touched her, she gasped out. And then he elicited another gasp when he poked forward until only the head of his lust-hardened shaft was hidden within.

"Yes, oh, yes, that. That's what I want!"

"No," he said. "That' not what you want. This is what you want. What we both need."

His hips moved forward in a smooth motion, carrying him to the hilt in her moist tightness. Her legs rose on either side of his body and he lifted her rump again off the floor. For a moment, he hung suspended, time and place vanished. All that mattered was the woman, her nearness, her tightness. He slowly withdrew, only to slip back quickly into her needy core.

Claudia began to thrash about under him. He gripped her fleshy buttocks and held her in place as he continued to thrust forward quickly and withdraw with taunting slowness. She tossed her head from side to side, eyes closed, biting her lower lip as she moaned in desire.

When the heat within Slocum's groin reached the point of burning him, he began to lose control of the steady movements. He began thrusting faster and generating carnal heat that released Claudia's desires. She cried out in joy, tensed around him, and made him feel as if she were milking him. He grunted, then began to piston back and forth even faster. The heat from her and the strength of the muscles surrounding him robbed him of the last of his control.

He spilled his white-hot seed in a rush. Then he sank down atop her until their faces were only inches apart.

"You're wonderful," she whispered.

"You're no so bad yourself," he replied.

"I'm not bad? I thought I was being positively wicked. We'll have to work on that and see if you can't make me into a completely wanton woman."

He rolled over beside her, and she came into his strong arms. There was a muzzy warmth that settled over him, but he still heard a scraping sound. Slocum sat up and looked around. Nothing.

Then Claudia got her second wind and moved to convince him to pick up where they had left off.

14

"Get dressed," Slocum said, craning around and not seeing the painting by the mouth of the cave where he had left it. He grabbed for his gun belt and pulled his six-shooter.

"What's wrong?" Claudia began buttoning her blouse, leaving her naked below the waist, but Slocum wasn't distracted right now. He was too busy getting his own jeans on and padding to see if the thief was in view.

"The painting's gone," Slocum said. He fastened the gun belt to his waist and shoved the six-gun into it. He felt disgust at his own weakness and how he had given in to Claudia's charms. Slocum didn't regret what he and Claudia had just done, but was furious at himself for giving anyone the chance to sneak so close and make off with the map.

"Who? Who took it?"

"I don't know," Slocum said, getting into his boots, "but the best way of finding out is to follow the tracks."

"I don't see anything."

"I don't either. Whoever swiped the painting did it sometime back when we were both occupied."

"The painting's gone!" Claudia almost whined. "We have to get it back!"

"Where's the paintbrush?"

"Here—oh, no, John! It's gone too!"

"Reckon that limits the folks who might have stolen them," Slocum said. "Neale might take the painting, but he'd also plug both of us. He's that kind of man." Slocum felt a cold anger at this. If Neale had found them, he would have used one bullet to shoot both of them while they were making love. He would have enjoyed the irony.

"Who?"

"I partnered up with the bounty hunter."

"Wilmer?"

"None other than," Slocum said, settling his gun belt. "I saved his worthless life, we threw our lots together, and now he double-crossed me. The lure of gold was too much for him."

"But Wilmer? That smelly person back at the Rio Grande gorge?"

"He knew about the painting and the brush," Slocum said. "He could have shot us both, but didn't. That's the best I can expect from a former partner." Slocum felt an anger he hadn't felt in years. Marshal Hanks mistakenly coming for him was one thing, but having someone betray him like this who had called himself partner and had shaken on it—that was about the same as horse stealing.

"You trusted him? Why?" Claudia stared at him incredulously.

"I saved his life and thought he owed me some loyalty. I was wrong about him."

"What do we do now?" Claudia pressed close, reminding him of the sort of reward she could offer. Right now, Slocum was less interested in sampling flesh and more inclined to spill blood.

"There's the way he went. For a mountain man, he didn't try covering his tracks. Maybe he didn't think there was any reason." Even as he said those words, a cold lump formed in Slocum's belly. "Son of a bitch!" he cried. Tearing out, he slipped and slid down the hillside, tumbled into the arroyo, and ignored Claudia's cries for him to wait for her. Getting his feet under him, Slocum sprinted to where the horses had been tethered.

Had been tethered.

Slocum stood with his arms dangling at his sides when Claudia ran up, out of breath.

"John," she gasped out. "What's wrong, John?"

"He stole my horse. The lowdown, no-account mangy son of a poxy whore stole my horse."

"And the painting."

Slocum looked at her sharply. She didn't understand. Slocum had been betrayed far worse than having the painting stolen out from under his nose. That rankled, but Wilmer had taken his horse. Slocum had called him partner, and Wilmer had betrayed him at every turn.

"How much did you leave in the cave?"

"Nothing I can't leave," she said, her eyes wide. She had never seen such towering anger before. "We . . . we should get started."

"You stay. I'll find him. It won't be pretty. You wouldn't want to see it, what I'll do to him."

"What's that, John? What will you do?"

"I've learned things from the Apaches, but what I'll do to Wilmer would make them turn white in fear."

He cast around and found the trail leading back to the road above. If Slocum had to make a guess, Wilmer had overheard Claudia say she had hunted for the gold in the three mines and had come up empty-handed. He would likely take the painting to the meadow and try to decipher it back there in comfort, with water and grass for his horse and all the time in the world to decipher the clues locked in the painting's brush strokes. Wilmer was nothing if not totally sure of his own abilities. The painting would be the perfect proof of it—if he figured out where the Army payroll had been hidden.

Without looking to see if Claudia came, he trudged up

the slope and got to the road. The fresh hoofprints showed
where two horses had come. Slocum recognized a nick in
one horseshoe as belonging to the horse he had ridden.

"Wait, John. I can't keep up."

Slocum saw the woman struggling up the slope carrying
supplies from the wrecked buckboard. He relented, went
back down the slope, and helped her to the road. The supplies would come in handy if Wilmer led them a long
chase. Slocum doubted that would happen since the bounty
hunter's arrogance was such that he would never expect
Slocum to come after him because of Claudia.

Slocum might show the trappings of a Southern gentleman, but when it came down to remaining with a lovely
lady or putting an ounce of lead into a horse thief's hide,
the only decision Slocum need make now was how hard to
squeeze back on the trigger.

"You are angry at him, aren't you? I . . . I haven't seen
this side of you before, John."

"Can you carry all that or do you want help? I would
prefer to keep my hands free in case I have to fire fast."

"I can lug it along just fine, thank you," she said
sharply. Claudia's lips thinned to a line as she made her
displeasure obvious to him. Her irritation was like water
on a duck's back to Slocum. There was only one thing on
his mind: revenge.

Slocum swung back and headed to the meadow that had
become a second home to him. When he got his horse back
and settled the score with Wilmer, he would ride to the far
side of the meadow, find the way through the mountains,
and get the hell out of New Mexico.

"Not so fast, John. I can hardly keep up."

Slocum slowed and let her draw even with him. He realized she was giving him good advice, even if it wasn't exactly what she'd meant. If he bulled his way out of the
canyon into the meadowland, he was likely to present a fine
target for Wilmer. The bounty hunter hadn't killed him and

Claudia before, but when he saw them on his trail, he wouldn't hesitate. An even deeper thorn dug into Slocum's soul. Wilmer was likely to shoot him down and try to claim he was Neale to collect the reward. Not only would Wilmer end up with the gold, he would get the bounty posted by the Army.

"I don't know why I'm going with you to that terrible place," Claudia said. "It has bad memories for me, what with Maggie's grave being there and all."

"How do you suppose she ended up dead?"

"She must have stolen the gold from Neale and hidden it."

"How'd your pa come to do the map then? Were he and Maggie in cahoots?"

"I . . . I never thought of that. He favored her. A little. A little over me," Claudia said. "She might have been too hurt to get away, and my pa buried her. Then he hid the gold and sent me the painting."

"Why didn't he just hightail it away with the gold?"

"Oh, John, you ask too many questions. I like you better when your mouth's engaged in . . . other ways." She batted her eyelashes in his direction. The violet light in her eyes blazed hotly, but Slocum wondered which of his questions had stung her most. From the way she acted, it had to do with the way her father and her sister got along.

Thicker than thieves and *blood is thicker than water* kept running through Slocum's mind.

He jerked straight, hand flying to his six-shooter when he heard gunfire ahead.

"Stay back. Get up in those rocks and don't poke your head up until I call you."

"I don't want to leave your side," Claudia protested.

More shots were followed by a loud, anguished cry that sapped Claudia's determination. She dropped the supplies she carried and dashed for rocks above the road. Slocum glanced around, got his bearings, and then cut off the road in the other direction, finding a less exposed route into the meadow. He crouched behind a blackberry bush and waited until the fight revealed where the combatants were.

It took only seconds for Slocum to see four riders prowling, rifles leveled and ready to fire if they saw anyone. Slocum didn't doubt they were in Neale's gang, although he didn't recall having seen them before.

All speculation vanished when Neale rode out, pointing, angrily shouting and dispatching the men to different areas in the meadow to cut off escape back into the canyon Slocum had just left. Watching and waiting, Slocum wanted one of those sentries to come close enough so he could plug the outlaw and get a new horse and maybe a rifle. If he wanted to have his revenge on Wilmer, he could use more firepower.

Rising, moving to put a pine tree between him and the outlaw riding slowly along the edge of the forest, Slocum drew his gun and sneaked a quick look around the trunk. The outlaw spotted him. Before he could yell out a warning to his friends, the road agent made a terrible mistake. He swung his rifle around to get a shot off.

Slocum shot first. The outlaw grunted, dropped his rifle, and clutched at his horse's neck as he bent forward. Before Slocum could get a second, killing shot off, the horse bolted and raced away.

Moving from the safety of the pine tree, he scooped up the rifle. Slocum looked around to see if he had been spotted. There was no way the gunshot would be overlooked—except for the fusillade coming from a hundred yards away that drowned out even the wounded outlaw's departure.

Slocum saw Wilmer ducking and dodging, firing his rifle as he made his way into the open. The bounty hunter was on foot and would never make it to cover with three outlaws riding him down. Slocum couldn't let Neale's gang kill Wilmer. He wanted to do that himself. Slocum raised the rifle, sighted, squeezed, and fired. One outlaw jerked around as the slug caught him high on the shoulder.

It wasn't a killing shot, but forced the man to drop his rifle. Slocum swung about, got a second shot off, and smiled with grim satisfaction when the outlaw tumbled from horseback. He might not be dead, but he wasn't going to be a factor in the fight.

Seeing two of his companions wounded, the third turned tail and galloped off, shouting at the top of his lungs for the rest of the gang.

"Slocum?" Wilmer stumbled and fell to his knees. Slocum began walking toward the bounty hunter, bringing the rifle to his shoulder as he went. His finger drew back on the trigger, but it fell with a metallic click. The magazine had come up empty.

Reaching for his six-shooter to finish the task, Slocum hesitated. From the woods on the far side of the clearing came a half-dozen outlaws.

"My God, Slocum, don't fire on 'em. It's too far for a pistol." Wilmer scampered about and grabbed both rifles dropped by the wounded outlaws. Running clumsily, he made a beeline for Slocum. Only the fact that the bounty hunter had two rifles and that Neale had spotted him kept Slocum from gunning Wilmer down.

"Here, catch," the bounty hunter said, tossing one rifle to Slocum. "You got a place where we can hold 'em off?"

"The trees," Slocum said, indicating the thorny undergrowth where he had hidden earlier.

"Ain't much but it'll have to do. Neale ambushed me."

"Fancy that. Bet he stole your horse too. And mine," Slocum said.

Wilmer didn't hear the sarcasm in Slocum's voice.

"Yep, he snuck up on me whilst I was eatin'. Got both horses and the painting. That son of a bitch's got the painting."

"He'll have our lives if we don't take cover," Slocum said, involuntarily ducking when a slug passed within inches of his left ear. He brought the rifle Wilmer had given him to his shoulder, aimed, and caused a similar re-action in one outlaw. The rider veered and ran into the outlaw on his left, causing a great confusion that let Slocum and Wilmer find spots behind sturdy tree trunks to make their stand.

"You're a peach, Slocum, savin' me like this. Don't know how you got here, but it's in the nick of time."

Slocum needed Wilmer if he was to get away from Neale and his gang. Otherwise, he would have put a slug in the bounty hunter's head then and there. He reminded himself as he began firing that he had to keep one round for Wilmer. If Neale was going to overrun them, Slocum wanted to be the one killing the bounty hunter for betraying him the way he had.

"The painting's in his hands now. Damn. Don't know how I coulda been so careless."

"The same thought occurred to me," Slocum said. He fired with enough accuracy to force away the attack Neale tried to launch. The outlaws fell back to a spot out of range for accurate firing. Slocum wasn't going to expend his ammo on anything but a clean shot.

"They'll try to circle us, come at us from two different directions at once. Might even try to sneak around behind us," Wilmer said, his neck craning about as he studied the forested area and the clearing in front of them. "They got enough men fer that. Must be ten in Neale's gang. I seen 'im but couldn't get a shot at 'im."

"He caught you flatfooted," Slocum said. "Admit it. He rode up, and you never knew he was within a mile of your camp."

"You don't know how it was."

From Wilmer's tone, Slocum knew exactly how it was. Wilmer had been gloating over his theft of the painting and horses and hadn't expected anyone to ride up on him. It had been his bad luck Neale had found him so easily.

"Where's the painting?"

"Back in those trees yonder," Wilmer said. "Ain't gonna do no good lookin', though. I'm sure Neale's already got it. No idea what he did with it."

"You have any more ammo?"

"Only what's in the rifles." Wilmer fired a couple of rounds, then lowered the rifle and looked over at Slocum. "Tell me somethin', will you?"

"I still want your scalp for stealing my horse."

It was as if Wilmer hadn't heard him. The bounty hunter asked, "Did that doxy actually search all three of them mines?"

"She did and she didn't find a thing."

"Do you believe her?"

"She wouldn't have been holed up in a cave, trying to figure out something else from the painting, if she'd found the gold. She would have taken it and been long gone."

"Yer right 'bout that. She'd have been long gone with the gold," Wilmer said.

"Glad you agree."

Again Slocum's sarcasm fell on deaf ears. Wilmer fell back to crouch beside Slocum.

"We got to get out of here. They'll be all over us 'fore we know it. We kin—"

"Listen," Slocum said.

"No, you listen, Slocum. I—" Wilmer fell silent, canted his head, and then slowly turned. He dropped flat on his belly and pressed his ear against the ground. After listening almost a minute, he looked up in admiration. "I declare, you got it all figgered out, don't ya, Slocum? There's not a sound of anything stirrin' out there."

The outlaws had left.

15

"Danged horse thieves," grumbled Wilmer. Slocum glared at the man and forced himself to keep from drawing his six-shooter and emptying all the chambers into him. He was a fine one to talk about stealing another man's horse. If anything, Slocum thought, Neale was only taking back the horse abandoned by the outlaw Slocum had killed earlier. But that had been a fair fight, and the outlaw wasn't going to use the animal anymore.

"The painting's gone too?"

"I had it hung up in that there tree, danglin' on a limb jist like it was in one of them galleries up in Denver. You ever see one of 'em, Slocum? They got entire halls filled with nuthin' but paintings and statues and people gawkin' at 'em. Never seen anything like it in all my born days."

"Art," Slocum said, walking through the camp and reconstructing what had happened. It didn't come as any surprise that Wilmer wasn't lying about any of it. More of the blue paint had rubbed off on the limb where he had hung the painting, and the number of horses that had come through the camp numbered at least five. Slocum wasn't going to argue if Wilmer said Neale and nine others had ridden in on him. But there was something missing in the bounty hunter's telling of the tale.

"Did they try to shoot you after you told them about the painting?" Slocum asked.

"That's what made me so mad. I—" Wilmer swung around and his eyes narrowed to slits. "What'd you say?"

"They snuck up on you, all right," Slocum said. "They caught you and were going to ventilate you, but a little dickering or a lot of shouting made Neale stop. You told him there was a map in the painting, didn't you?"

"They was gonna kill me, Slocum! What else could a man do?"

"The painting's not going to help Neale any," Slocum said, recollecting the trouble he and Claudia had had trying to decipher the puzzle. And he'd had the advantage of working with another artist, one whose father had drawn the painting.

"He don't know that," said Wilmer.

"He might figure it out mighty quick that he needs more information," Slocum said. "When he does, he might decide to come looking for you again." He motioned to the bounty hunter to follow him.

"Where we goin'?"

"Claudia's up in the canyon. We have to tell her what happened."

"Why? She done real good on her own before. We kin—"

"We can find her," Slocum said, again considering if he ought to expend all six of his bullets on Wilmer. The idea was turning attractive again. The bounty hunter must have read it in his eyes because his shaggy head started bobbing up and down like it was on a spring.

"All right, we kin do that. We oughta tell her Neale's done stole her painting."

Slocum trooped off, marveling at how easy it was for Wilmer to place the blame elsewhere. If he hadn't stolen the painting from the cave while Slocum and Claudia were otherwise occupied, Neale could never have come into possession of the painting.

Footsore and fuming, Slocum finally got to the spot where he had shooed Claudia into the rocks. He looked around and didn't see her.

"We gotta keep movin', Slocum. How long's it gonna take Neale to realize he don't know squat about that painting and the map? When he gits all het up, he'll come chargin' after us."

Slocum ignored the bounty hunter and cupped his hands to his mouth and called, "Claudia! Get down here. We got to talk. Claudia!"

"She hidin' 'round here? We don't need that—" Wilmer cut off his sentence when Claudia came slipping and sliding down the side of the hill.

"Why'd you bring *him* back? So I can rip his eyes out?" She glared at Wilmer. Slocum was amused at the way Wilmer averted his face like a guilty child caught stealing.

"We ended up saving each other's lives," Slocum said, not wanting to go into it. "Neale has the painting."

"I . . . I won't give up. Not that easily," she said. Claudia motioned Slocum over so she could have a private talk with him. "I remember every brush stroke on that painting, John. We don't need him. But I do need the paintbrush. Did you find it?"

Slocum shook his head. He had been too busy staying alive to hunt for the brush, but he didn't remember seeing it lying around Wilmer's camp.

"That's got to be the key," Claudia said urgently. "We can find it. Neale didn't steal it too, did he?"

"Wilmer, where's the paintbrush? You stole it when you took the painting."

"Brush? This here thing?" Wilmer reached around behind his back and wiggled. He whipped the brush around and flourished it like a sword.

"That," Slocum said, moving like a striking snake. He snared the brush before Wilmer could jerk it away. Slocum tossed it to Claudia. "What do you make of it?"

"I don't know. This arrow has to mean something."

"It oriented the map—the painting," Slocum said.

"There must be more, and I don't think it was on the painting, John. The brush *must* mean more."

Slocum turned to the mine he had singled out as being the one where the gold was most likely to have been hidden. He pointed to it and said, "You looked that hole in the ground over real good?"

"Yes," Claudia said. "All of them."

"You see anything out of the ordinary in that mine?"

"I can't think of anything. All three looked to have been deserted at the same time. The only thing different about that one was the way someone had carved squiggly lines all over the rock. Must have taken a while, but then what else do miners have to do with their spare time?"

"They ain't got spare time. If they was wantin' to dig in rock, it'd be for gold," Wilmer said. He caught Slocum's eye and inclined his head toward the mine on the far side of the canyon.

"Let's take a look at those carvings," Slocum said, leading the way. It took the better part of two hours for them to reach the mine. By this time Slocum was dog tired and Claudia could hardly walk. Only Wilmer bounced about like a child's ball, full of piss and vinegar. The only thing keeping Slocum moving along to the mine was the knowledge that he had gone to the meadow to kill Wilmer and could do so anytime he wanted.

Flopping down in the mouth of the mine, Slocum looked around. He didn't see the carved walls Claudia had mentioned.

"Not here, deeper inside. You think the gold might really be here?"

"I'm thinking this is a gold goose chase," Slocum said.

He had been right when he had considered forsaking the entire hunt as being nothing but a phantasm. That day seemed like it was a thousand years earlier and someone else had lived his life since.

"A thousand dollars of gold, Slocum," Wilmer said enticingly. "We kin find it. I know we kin."

Slocum heaved himself to his feet.

"Show me," he ordered Claudia.

"At the first bend in the mine, just where you couldn't see from the mouth." Claudia had swallowed some of Wilmer's enthusiasm. The lure of gold was powerful.

Slocum found the markings, fumbled in his pocket, and pulled out the tin holding his lucifers. He scratched one against the mine wall and let its flare die down before holding it close to the wall. Claudia was right. Fresh marks and peculiarly formed for anything a miner might do. Slocum tried to determine how the scratches could have been made accidentally, and saw no way.

"Whatya make of 'em, Slocum?" asked Wilmer.

"Bring that paintbrush over and get ready to put it into the middle of the scratches when I light another match."

Claudia and Wilmer pressed close as Slocum lit the wall again. Claudia did as she was told, then saw the faint outline of what might have been a brush, and hurriedly moved it between those lines.

"Son of a gun," muttered Slocum. "You see what I did?"

"A word, John, there's a word that's apparent when the center of the marks is covered by the brush."

"What's it? Tell me what it is," Wilmer said.

Slocum remembered that Wilmer was illiterate.

"The name Goggins mean anything to you?" Slocum lit another match as he watched Wilmer's face screw up in concentration. There was no sign Wilmer had ever heard the name.

"How about you?" Slocum asked Claudia.

"I . . . I think so," she said uncertainly. "Papa sent a

rambling letter along with the painting and said something about someone named Goggins. A miner?"

"The miner who blasted this shaft?" Slocum licked his fingers when the lucifer burned them. He retreated to the mouth of the mine and looked around. There wasn't even a miner's shack left. Someone had torn it down and used the wood for a fire. He walked to the firepit and kicked through the ashes until he found the corner of an old newspaper. He pulled it out and held it up.

"What's it say?" Wilmer peered at the paper, as if it would give him the location of the gold.

And Slocum realized it might do just that.

"If Goggins was the miner working this claim, he must have burned all this to stay warm before moving on. This likely tells us where he moved. It's from the *Las Vegas Optic*. Tells of a new strike in Sangre Canyon. You know where that is, Wilmer?"

"Reckon so," the bounty hunter said, tipping his head back as if he intended to sniff out the proper location. "I know these mountains better 'n I know my own hand."

"That's because you've never scraped off all that dirt," Claudia said, so low that the bounty hunter couldn't hear. Slocum repressed a smile. Then the smile died.

"You said you were all mixed up when it came to these canyons," Slocum said.

"Never. Not me. This here Sangre Canyon's jist over the top of the rise. We kin hike it in an hour and then see what's bein' mined on the far side."

Slocum looked at Claudia, who silently nodded. The gold still put a spring in her step. Heaving a deep sigh, Slocum set off to find the best way up and over the top into the next canyon.

The rain started just as they crested the top. Slocum wasn't sure where it had come from, but the storm came fast and out of a sky that had been clear of clouds only minutes earlier.

"We've got to get under cover," he shouted at Claudia and Wilmer. "We'll be washed down the side of the mountain if we don't."

"Need to find that miner," Wilmer insisted. "You ain't turnin' fancy boy on me, are you, Slocum? Little rain scare you off?"

"This isn't little," Claudia protested. "I can't even see my hand in front of my face."

"Don't need sight to track. You do it by instinct, same as I do."

"The stink's being washed off you, all right," Claudia said, keeping her head down. Slocum saw how the rain had soaked her clothing through and through. He wasn't complaining about that since her clothing clung to her sleek, trim body like a second skin, but they had to get out of this frog-strangler. Most mountain storms passed quick.

"There's got to be a mine somewhere around. Find it," he told Wilmer, "if you're so damn good. Who knows? It might even be Goggins'."

Wilmer paced back and forth, every footstep causing mud to splash up under his heavy tread. He stopped and pointed into the curtain of gray rain.

"That way. Let's go."

Claudia looked at Slocum questioningly.

"Doesn't much matter if he's right," Slocum said. "One direction's as good as any other until we find shelter."

They trooped for less than ten minutes, slipping on the increasingly slick rocks, until a wooden structure appeared through the sheets of rain pelting them.

"Tole ya I'd find somewhere to get out of the rain," Wilmer gloated. He held open the door for Claudia, then ducked in ahead of Slocum.

"It's almost as wet in here as outside," Claudia said. "The roof is leaking like a sieve."

"Take care of that in a second," Wilmer said, stepping

onto a stool. He rattled the roof a few times, then took a piece of canvas Slocum handed him and tucked it into place so the rain caught in the folds and dripped into a corner of the single-room shack.

"That'll work for a while," Slocum said, sitting down on the only chair.

"I don't like this place," Claudia said. She glanced at Wilmer and wrinkled her nose, making it clear what part of the shack she didn't like. The bounty hunter smelled like a wet dog.

"When the rain quits, we keep lookin' fer this Goggins fella, right?" Wilmer kicked the stool closer to Slocum and sat down on it, leaving Claudia standing. She looked around for something to sit on, and finally perched on the edge of the table after seeing how soaked the thin pallet that passed for a bed was.

"What's he likely to tell us that we don't already know?" asked Slocum. "We should have found the gold back on the other side of the mountain, if it even exists."

"Of course it exists," insisted Wilmer. "Yer thinkin' on how you got that gold coin off one of Neale's boys, ain't you?"

"The thought was festering," Slocum admitted.

"That don't mean it came from the payroll," Wilmer insisted, "and it prob'ly didn't 'cuz Neale wanted the painting fer somethin' more than to hang over the fireplace in his house."

Slocum had no answer for that, but he still didn't know what Goggins could tell them, if they had deciphered the message properly. Everything was too tenuous to grab. Slocum was beginning to think the gold was long gone and he ought to be also. Only, he had no horse or supplies. If he found the gold before he got a horse, good. Otherwise, he was clearing out.

His hand flashed to his six-shooter and he drew, the muzzle aimed at the door as it creaked open to reveal a man.

"Whatcha doin' in my place?"

"Who're you?" Slocum stood, keeping his six-gun pointed at the man's midsection. When the man slipped inside and closed the door, Slocum got a better look at him. He was dressed as a miner, and they had invaded his shack.

"Name's Goggins," came the answer. "And you kin stay till the rain's done with, then you go. Ain't nobody allowed on my claim."

"Mr. Goggins!" cried Claudia, jumping to her feet. "You knew my father. You knew Kenneth Peterson!"

"Who might you be, missy?" Goggins shambled closer and peered at Claudia from only a few inches away. His smile lit up the room. "You must be Kenny's other daughter. I been expectin' you."

"Why's that?" asked Slocum, but he knew the answer.

"I reckoned you'd be comin' fer the gold eventually. Too much of it fer ya not to come on by to take a gander at it."

"Where is it? It's ours!" Wilmer got off the stool and went toward the miner. Slocum held the bounty hunter back with the barrel of his Colt.

"Seems to me you're mighty happy to part with that information," Slocum said to Goggins. Something wasn't right.

"Could be, could be," Goggins said, stroking his stubbled chin. "A damn shame what happened to your pappy."

"What? What happened to him? I keep expecting to see him come riding up and—"

"Sorry, missy, 'fraid I gotta tell you that ain't gonna happen. He got killed by them outlaws. The ones led by the deserter from Fort Union."

"Neale? Neale killed my father?"

"Shot him right down when he wouldn't fess up to what he did with the gold. That outlaw's got the worst temper I ever seen in any man."

"How'd Maggie get killed?" Slocum grew increasingly uneasy with the old miner.

"She stole the gold from Neale. Neale upped and hijacked a gold shipment made by the Army, but she stole it out from under his nose. He killed her in one humongous towerin' rage. Shot her right down not too far from here."

"Why'd he bury her body?" Slocum shot a look at both Claudia and Wilmer to keep them quiet. The gold wasn't going anywhere. He needed to know how it had come to be hidden before his worry would quiet down.

"Didn't. Kenny buried her when he found her. Saw it all, I did." Goggins coughed and spat into the corner of the room. From the look of the wood in the walls, he used this corner exclusively as a spittoon. "Neale found him after he finished plantin' her all proper-like, but 'fore he could even put a marker on the grave."

"And Kenneth Peterson told you where he hid the gold after Maggie gave it to him?"

"Well, now, that's not perzactly what happened. But him and me, we done roamed these hills together fer a spell, me prospectin' and him dabbin' paint on that canvas of his. He made me promise to tell his daughter—that'd be you, missy—what I know if 'n anything happened to him."

"Why didn't he just tell Claudia to find you instead of sending the painting and making her jump through hoops like some circus animal to even find you?"

"Cain't say. Kenny was a strange bird."

"Where's the damn gold?" Wilmer exploded after holding back the only question of interest to him.

The miner started to speak when Slocum felt the ground shift under his feet. Then the rain cascaded down on him from the canvas and the entire shack collapsed. He was flung back by a wall of water racing from higher up on the hill, and then flailed as he was washed down the mountainside.

16

"John!"

Slocum heard Claudia screaming, but couldn't get to his feet. Splintery wood planks cut at his face and hands, forcing him to raise an arm to protect himself. As he did, a new torrent of water came washing down with the force of a battering ram and hit him full in the chest, bowling him over and sending him crashing through the downhill side of the shack. The impact stunned him. He tumbled and rolled, somersaulting and trying to get his balance. The wall of water embraced him, held him, threw him farther down the mountain.

"John, help me! I can't swim!"

Slocum heard Claudia's words in the far distance, as if she were riding a train and disappearing into a tunnel. He almost laughed. Swimming had nothing to do with staying alive in this flood. No one could swim in this. No one could survive it. Slocum's head hit a rock and it dazed him—and he kept riding the tide downhill.

"Gotcha, gotcha, Slocum."

He heard the words, but the grip on his shoulder failed. He was soaked through and through and the power of the water hurtling down to the bottom of the canyon was too

great to resist. Slocum finally stopped fighting the water
and tried to roll with it. Eventually, after an eternity, he
flopped out flat on his belly, shaken and gasping for breath.

He pushed up to his hands and knees, still blinded by
the driving rain. The torrent had passed, but the sky had
opened up and kept pelting him with watery fists hard
enough to drive him back flat on the ground. A cactus under his belly prompted him to roll to the side and get away
from the pain it caused.

Slocum finally sat up, plucked out the nettles, and then
struggled to his feet.

"Slocum, help. I cain't move!"

Wilmer's call caused him to pivot and home in on the
sound of the bounty hunter's voice. Through the rain he
saw the man clinging to a splinter of rock. Sheer terror
was etched on Wilmer's face. This more than anything
else got Slocum moving to his aid. When he got closer,
Slocum saw the reason for the man's fright. His feet dangled over a sheer drop. If his arms lost their death grip
around the needle of rock, he would plunge down more
than thirty feet.

"Git me up 'fore more rain washes down from above,"
pleaded Wilmer.

Slocum sized up the situation, cautiously edged forward, and planted his feet against rocks that seemed secure. He used both hands to grab one of Wilmer's wrists.

"Pull, damn your eyes, Slocum, pull! I cain't hold on no
longer!"

Even as the words slipped from his mouth, the bounty
hunter's strength disappeared. Slocum suddenly supported
the man entirely, his grip on Wilmer's wrist slipping instant to instant because of the rain. He dug in his heels,
bent his legs, and heaved with all his might. Wilmer flew
up in the air and landed on solid ground like a fish pulled
out of a stream.

"Dang, Slocum, that was close. Too close." Wilmer hazarded a look toward what would have been his fate, then shuddered and turned his head.

"Get away from the edge. I can't fling you around like that again. I'm all tuckered out." Slocum pulled his hat down farther on his forehead and blocked most of the rain aiming to blind him as he backed away from the cliff.

"Don't see gully-washers like that too often, but enough," Wilmer said, picking his way from the verge and finally dropping down with a huge boulder between him and the drop-off.

Slocum looked around in the driving rain for Claudia, but couldn't see her. He called her name, but got nothing but distant echoes of the rain pounding into the rock as an answer. He'd started to make his way back up the steep slope when he felt Wilmer's heavy hand on his leg.

"Where you goin'?"

"To find Claudia. If we were washed down the hill, what would have happened to her?" He and Wilmer were strong enough to fight the water—a little—and survive. Claudia was burdened by heavy skirts and had nowhere near the strength required to hang on against that torrent of water gushing downhill.

"You're goin' in the wrong direction to find her," Wilmer said. He jerked his thumb back over his shoulder. "She'd have been washed over the cliff."

"You don't know that."

"Go on, waste yer time and energy," Wilmer said. "It's hard enough to sit in the rain. Fightin' it's a damn fool thing to do, Slocum, and you know it. Set yerself down and wait it out. You'll find her quicker after the rain's petered out."

"What about Goggins? He knows where the gold is hidden."

"He don't know squat. If he knew where Peterson hid the payroll, he'd've been out of here like he was plumb shot from a cannon—with the gold makin' his damn pockets bulge."

"He's not staying because of the mining," Slocum said, reluctantly agreeing. The abandoned mines on all the hillsides were mute testament to how little pay dirt had been removed from this area of the Sangre de Cristo Mountains.

"Why'd Peterson go and scratch Goggins' name into the mine wall like he done?" Wilmer pulled up his legs and hid his face between his knees to protect himself from the incessant rain.

Slocum chewed over what the bounty hunter had said. It all made sense, and yet none of it did. Had Goggins been searching every single mine for the hidden gold? That sounded like about the stupidest thing Slocum could conceive of—unless Goggins had some clue to the hiding place and was trying to locate it. With the painting, or with Claudia, he might have the final piece of the puzzle.

"We've got to find Claudia," Slocum said, getting to his feet. As slick as the rocks were, he made his way through the rain to the destroyed shack. All he found were flinders. The wall of water had struck the shack and split it into two roughly equal segments. He and Wilmer had been washed one way while Goggins and Claudia had gone off at an angle. Constantly wiping the rain from his face, Slocum stared into the gray gloom in the direction Claudia had been carried away. He hated to admit that the bounty hunter was probably right. Claudia would have been washed over the cliff.

He walked a few paces and stared at the ground. The heavy rain had washed away any trace of Claudia's or Goggins's tracks. The deep gully carved into the hillside was his only guide as he made his way lower, angling farther from the cliff as he went. Hope soared. Claudia might have avoided a plunge to her death.

The incline was steep, but not a sheer cliff, as Slocum went ever lower and eventually came out in the canyon below. He pulled down his hat brim to protect his eyes as he looked back. He caught glimpses of the terrain now that the rain was letting up a mite. Heaving a sigh, he began hunting for Claudia on the canyon floor. When he reached the spot at the base of the cliff where Wilmer had dangled, he looked up.

The rain was about over.

"Wilmer!" he shouted. "You still up there? I'm below, looking for Claudia and the prospector."

He waited, but the bounty hunter didn't poke his shaggy head over the edge of the cliff. Slocum shrugged it off. Wilmer had a fear of heights, he figured, especially this one after he had nearly plunged to his death off the precipice. He turned back to hunting for any trace of Claudia, but eventually gave up. The rain had permanently eroded the landscape and washed huge boulders lower on the mountainside. There wasn't any track Claudia could have left that would have survived such a downpour.

Slocum squeezed as much of the water from his shirt as he could, and his boots squished as he walked. This didn't stop him from prowling about as he hunted for Claudia. He called a few more times, but got no answer. The smaller animals were finally poking their heads out of their burrows to see how the rain had changed their homes. He considered taking a rock to the head of a rabbit and fixing a fire. Rabbit meat and warmth seemed like a good combination.

If he were lucky, the odor of roasting meat would bring Claudia and Goggins running. If Lady Luck turned on him, he could attract Neale and his gang.

Before he could do much in the way of hunting for dinner, he caught sight of a piece of cloth fluttering on a prickly pear spine. Slocum snatched it up from the tangle of nettles and looked at it closely. It had been torn from Claudia's skirt. He spun in a full circle, then examined the ground. If she had passed this way after the rainstorm, her tracks would be obvious, even on the rocky stretches all around.

Slocum laughed with joy when he saw distinct footprints, just the right size to be Claudia's, leading back in the direction of the meadow. That wasn't a smart way to go with Neale and his gang patrolling there, but she might not know where she was. Try as he might, Slocum couldn't find any spoor showing that Goggins was still with her.

Trooping along the gravelly bank proved the easiest way of travel. Thick streams still flowed in the bottom of the usually dry arroyo as more runoff from the hundreds of square miles of solid rock poured through the canyon.

"Slocum? That you?"

Slocum's hand went to his Colt Navy; then he checked the draw when he saw Wilmer making his way through the debris left by the storm.

"I thought you were going to stay on the mountain," Slocum said.

"Changed my mind. A fella can do that, can't he?"

Something about Wilmer's attitude made Slocum edgy. The bounty hunter was defiant and wouldn't look him in the eye.

"What'd you find?"

"Didn't find nuthin'. How about you?"

Slocum held up the piece torn from Claudia's skirt. Wilmer scowled as he turned it over and over in his hand, fingers rubbing intimately against it.

"Yep, that's hers. She headin' back to the meadowlands?"

"Don't know if Goggins is with her," Slocum said, turning to look ahead. He stumbled and fell to his knees when Wilmer clubbed him with a piece of wood washed down from higher in the canyon. Slocum tried to pull out his six-shooter, but Wilmer hit him a second time, this blow landing on Slocum's upper right arm. Needles of pain danced the entire length as his hand numbed and his fingers refused to grasp the ebony butt. A third blow crashed into the middle of Slocum's back. He fell facedown on the wet ground.

"Sorry 'bout this, Slocum. Cain't see any profit in stayin' around much longer. Especially not now. Not when . . ."

Slocum thought the bounty hunter's words faded away, but he was dimly aware that he was losing consciousness. He held on grimly, refusing to black out. Whatever Wilmer was up to had to be stopped.

Through the roaring in his ears, Slocum heard Wilmer call out, "Over here. I got 'im here."

The clop-clop of hooves approached. Slocum turned a little and wiped dirt from his eyes to see Marshal Hanks riding up, a shotgun resting in the crook of his arm. He could swing that around and cut Slocum in half before the Colt could be dragged from its holster.

"You did get him, didn't you?" the marshal said in amazement. "I woulda spent the rest of my natural life trackin' the bastard. He alive?"

"Yep, that he is, Marshal."

Hanks sounded a tad bitter about it when he said, "Then you git the hunnerd dollars."

"Now? Do I git it now, Marshal? I want to be on my way soon as I kin move my cracker ass outta these mountains."

"Suppose it'd be all right," Hanks said. "Here's the money. Now where's the varmint's horse?"

"Ain't got one, Marshal. I don't neither, but I been walkin' all my life and I aim to keep doin' so."

"Then git to puttin' one foot in front of the other," Hanks said. "I got some interrogatin' to do."

"What do you mean?"

"Questions, Wilmer, I got questions to ask of Mr. Neale."

"Not Neale," Slocum grated out. "I keep telling you that. I'm not Neale."

"Shut up," Wilmer said, a note of desperation in his voice. He didn't want Slocum convincing the marshal he wasn't the outlaw leader. That would destroy his chances of collecting the hundred-dollar reward. Worse, Slocum was sure the bounty hunter would plug him and collect the twenty-five dollars rather than lose everything. Better a dead imitator than a living one able to convince the marshal he had the wrong man.

"Here's your bounty," the lawman said. Slocum saw a brown blur as a small leather bag was tossed through the air. Wilmer caught it deftly, peered inside, then tucked it away.

"Much obliged, Marshal. Hope the hangin' goes quick."

"It'd better," Slocum snarled. "You won't be able to run far enough." He grunted when Wilmer kicked him in the ribs.

"Hey, don't go damagin' the goods," Hanks piped up. "Git on outta here, Wilmer, 'fore I take you in for obstructin' justice."

"Nice doin' business with you, Marshal," Wilmer said.

Slocum fought to get to his feet. When he did, he was looking down the twin bores of the marshal's shotgun.

"Hand over that smoke wagon of yers, Neale."

"I'm not Neale. My name's Slocum. I—"

"Shut up. Mosey on over to those trees. Do it or I'll hogtie and drag you."

Slocum did as he was told. Hanks dismounted, stuffed Slocum's Colt and holster into his saddlebags, and then followed.

"Set yerse'f down and put your hands behind you."

The marshal was expert at tying up prisoners. Slocum's hands were secured, and then the lawman worked on his feet. When he was finished, Slocum couldn't hardly wiggle, much less put up a fuss when the questions began flying.

"You hid that payroll, Neale," Hanks said. "Make it easy on yerse'f and tell me where it is."

"Even if I were Neale, I wouldn't tell you. You'd just steal it for yourself."

Slocum barely turned to avoid the worst of the blow Hanks delivered to his jaw.

"Don't go mouthin' off," the lawman ordered. "You'll only make this worse 'fore it's over."

"You ever intend to take me back to Las Vegas?"

"You gotta stand trial. It'll go easier if you confess and let me turn back the gold to the Army." He hit Slocum again, knocking him to the ground. In this position, Slocum's ear pressed into the ground.

"Someone's coming," Slocum said, hearing the pounding of horses through the ground. "You might want to get ready. It's likely to be Neale or some of his gang."

Hanks took to high ground, dropping bell-down on a high rock. Slocum struggled against the ropes, but couldn't loosen those on his hands. The ropes binding his feet were a tad looser, but it would require a considerable amount of work to free himself. He doubted Hanks would give him the chance.

"Son of a bitch!" the marshal exclaimed.

Slocum propped himself up and saw what had brought the curse to the marshal's lips. Neale rode with two of his henchmen.

Slocum kept silent as the outlaws rode past not fifty feet away. He craned his neck around to get a look at Hanks, but the marshal was nowhere to be seen.

When Neale had disappeared, Hanks walked around the rock, looking shaken.

"Do you believe me now? My name's Slocum. *That's* the gent you want for the payroll robbery. That's Neale."

"You're the spittin' image of him, but—"

"But nothing!" raged Slocum. "He's getting away. He's the outlaw. He robbed the Army of its gold."

Hanks took a step toward him, looking confused. Then determination settled him down.

"You stay put," the marshal said. "I'll nab him and compare the two of you. I done paid fer you and I don't wanna make a mistake 'bout which of you is Neale."

"Let me go. You can't—" Slocum was talking to empty

air. Hanks had swung into the saddle and was foolishly trailing the three outlaws. In less than a minute he was gone from sight. In two minutes, Slocum heard galloping horses. In three, heavy gunfire. And in four, nothing. Nothing but the silence of the canyon after a heavy rain.

17

Slocum struggled to get free of the ropes holding his wrists behind his back, and couldn't. He rocked over until his hands were under him and began kicking. When a spur caught between two rocks, he began pulling slowly and got one foot out of its boot. It took him a few minutes to get his other foot free and the boots out of the ropes; then he began edging around to get his feet back in.

The sound of approaching riders made him reconsider. He left his boots where they were, struggled to get to his feet with his hands still bound, and stumbled barefoot to get to higher ground and find a hiding place. Slocum fell heavily, landing on one shoulder, when he heard Neale bark out, "There might be deputies. Give the whole area a good going-over, men."

"Ah, Neale, that marshal was too dumb to believe. He ain't got deputies with him. He was alone."

"Do it. I want to be sure."

The men with Neale grumbled but came prowling. Slocum wiggled like a worm to get entirely behind a rock before the outlaws spotted him. He succeeded, but the sharp-eyed road agents found his boots.

"Hey, Neale, come lookit this," one called to his boss.

"Got a pair of boots. Looks to have been tied together with rope."

Slocum sat up and fought even harder to get his hands free. Hanks might have been a fool when it came to chasing outlaws, but he was too good at tying knots. Getting to his feet, Slocum kept low and began working his way through the rocks in an attempt to get to higher ground so he wouldn't have the outlaws looking down on him. The rocky ground cut at his feet, but Slocum ignored the pain. It was better than what would happen if Neale spotted him.

"Think he might have hightailed it?" one outlaw asked his leader.

"Find out. Get on up there and hunt him down. Somebody's got to belong to those boots," Neale said. "I'll keep lookout down here in case you flush him."

Slocum cursed under his breath. Neale was too cagey. Moving heavily, Slocum wiggled into a fall of rocks and scared off a snake. He hardly noticed if it was a rattler or something less dangerous. Even a rattlesnake bite was better than Neale putting a bullet in his belly and leaving him to die.

"Be careful, Joe," one outlaw said to his partner. "We don't know if the gent's armed."

"How can he be? His feet was tied. Think the marshal did it? Might be one of the gang."

"Be good for joshin' around the campfire, if it is. Who you think it might be? That whore's son Dodge?"

"You know what he calls himself? Ice. Ice Dodge, he wants folks to call him, since he claims he's got ice water in his veins."

"He's afraid of Injuns, he's afraid of dogs, hell, he's afraid of his own shadow. Ice?" The outlaw laughed boisterously.

Slocum began dragging the ropes around his wrists against a rough-edged rock, but the surface abraded his skin more than the ropes. He felt his hands turning damp from blood flowing from cuts and scrapes.

"This way. I got a few dislodged rocks."

Slocum knew his time was almost up. Then a hand clamped around his mouth to keep him from crying out. It was a hand he recognized instantly and he shook his head, getting his mouth away from those slender fingers.

"Get me out of the ropes," he ordered Claudia. "Two of Neale's men are almost on top of us."

"I know," she said. "Wait a minute."

"We don't have that much time." He felt her sawing away at the ropes, and then his hands came free. He rubbed away the blood and shook his hands to get circulation back in them.

"Here, take this," she said, thrusting a knife into his hands.

"Where'd you get this?"

"Found it after I got washed away from the cabin. It must have been inside and got caught up in the water."

Slocum motioned for her to be quiet, started to push her down, and then reconsidered. He left Claudia where she was, in plain sight of anyone coming up the slope. Moving as fast as he could on his bare feet over the sharp rocks, he got out of sight just in time.

"Well, lookee here. And where'd you come from, little lady?"

The outlaw was overconfident and too engrossed in staring at Claudia and the way her clothing had been ripped as she was washed down the side of the mountain. Slocum regretted that this pleasant sight was the last thing the outlaw saw before being sent to hell with a quick slash of the knife across his throat. Before the man's dead body hit the ground, Slocum was yanking his pistol from its holster. He swung, fanned off three quick shots, and sent the second outlaw after the first.

"Grab that one's six-gun," Slocum barked to Claudia. He didn't wait to see if the woman obeyed. He was hobbling back downhill to have it out with Neale. But when

Slocum reached the spot where he had left his boots, he saw nothing of the road agent. Slocum dropped to the ground, picked out fragments of rock and spines from his feet, then pulled on his boots. He felt better for that, but wished he could find Neale.

"Wh-where is he?" Claudia gasped out. She waved the second outlaw's six-shooter around so much that Slocum reached out and took it from her. She looked relieved.

"He left his men. Don't know if he expects to come back or whether they were to meet up with him later." He grinned as a thought came to him. "Their horses. They left them around somewhere. Let's find them before the rest of the gang is breathing down our necks."

Slocum got to his feet and walked gingerly. He imagined the wounds leaking blood and filling his boots, but he ignored the pain as he hunted for the horses. It took him only a few minutes to find where they had been tethered.

"I'll be glad to get back in the saddle," he said.

"Where do we go now, John?"

"Somewhere we can hole up for a while. I don't want to stay out in plain sight much longer. Neale might have heard the shots."

"He'll think his men were doing the shooting."

"And then he'll wonder why they haven't reported back," Slocum finished for her. "We need to hide out for a spell." He rubbed his belly as it growled. "I need food too. It's been a while." Taking the canteen from its leather thong, he downed a goodly amount of water, wiped his lips, and felt better. Food in his belly would go even further toward making him feel like whipping his weight in wildcats. Or having it out with Neale.

"I . . . I see something yonder," Claudia said. "It might be a cave, but it's not too high up on the mountain."

"Better and better," Slocum said, seeing the spot she indicated. "We can put the horses inside with us."

They rode into the cave and found it more than large

enough for both the horses and themselves. Slocum pulled
off the saddles and handed the saddlebags set to Claudia.

"Fix us something to eat. No fire. I'll be back in a few
minutes."

"Where are you going?" She looked frightened.

"To cover our trail. Don't worry so." He kissed her, then
found it necessary to pry her loose as she clung to him.
Slocum left her behind, hoping she would do as he asked
and get some food ready. It took him more than a half hour
to properly destroy the hoofprints in the wet ground, but ju-
dicious use of rocks to cover part of the trail and a creosote
bush dragged repeatedly over the prints made it almost impossible to find where they had ridden.

When he got back, he found two cans of beans open and
waiting. Claudia huddled against one wall, legs drawn up
and her arms circling her knees.

"I didn't think you'd ever be back."

"What? And leave such a scrumptious meal?" His joke
fell on deaf ears. He picked up both cans and handed one to
her. She shook her head, but he insisted. She took the can
and stared into the mass of beans.

"Looks awful."

"Eat. We need to keep up our strength."

"For what?" She scooped out a few beans and impishly
smeared them on Slocum's face. He licked them off, then
did the same to her—but lower. The beans dripped down
into the deep crevice between her breasts. She started to
wipe the beans away, but Slocum caught her wrist.

"I'll do it," he said. He moved his face down lower, and
then pressed his lips against the woman's exposed chest.
Claudia sighed heavily, sending her bosoms up and down.
Slocum began licking up the sauce. One bean slid lower
and vanished. Slocum followed it down, his tongue flash-
ing out repeatedly.

"Oh, John," she sighed. She pushed away the flimsy
cloth covering her right breast. Slocum pounced on it and

sucked in the hard nub at the top. He tongued and sucked and then bit gently. Claudia gasped as he did so, her chest arching up to cram more of that succulent mound into his mouth.

He moved to the other breast, using his tongue to push away the cloth rather than having Claudia do it for him. He nuzzled and burrowed and when he was finished with it, worked his way even lower. The blouse, although torn, began to resist his advance.

Working his hand up under her skirt, he felt how her thigh quivered with anticipation. He pushed the unwanted cloth out of the way as he inched ever upward until he reached the furred nest between her thighs. One finger slipped wetly into her and began wiggling about.

"John, oh, I . . . I love the feel. But I want more."

He ignored her and kept licking at her chest. Using his other hand, he opened her blouse and let it hang open. This let him kiss his way lower to her belly button. His tongue drove down like a drill into the deep depression, then slipped out and circled around before moving lower. He reached a mountain of bunched-up skirt.

Slocum added a finger within her heated core and started stroking in and out. It felt as if all of Claudia's bones had turned to water. She sagged down onto the cave floor, stretching her arms high above her head and arching her hips upward so Slocum would have even better access to her most intimate regions. He took full advantage of this, moving so that his upper body was firmly between her thighs. His face only inches from the fragrant tangle nestled between her legs, Slocum took a moment to look up. Claudia's face was framed delightfully by her breasts.

Then he dived down, applying his mouth to the sweet pink gash while he kept his fingers moving within her. She let out a cry of pure delight, lifted her behind off the floor, and ground herself into his face. Slocum lapped and licked and stroked until Claudia was thrashing about in the throes of utter passion.

The passion mounted as he continued his oral assault, and then she let out a cry that echoed through the cave and must have been heard all the way to Las Vegas. Slocum never let up his tonguing and fingering until she sagged weakly to the floor. Then he abandoned his post and moved up her body until he loomed over her. He ran his hands under her ass and lifted until she pressed her crotch into his.

"Feel anything there?" he asked.

"Oh, yes, yes," she said, "but it's all hidden. Imprisoned."

"Free me," he ordered.

She reached between them and fumbled open his fly one button at a time. When he sprang out, her nimble fingers circled him and guided the purpled arrowhead directly to the spot where they both wanted it delivered. He hesitated a moment, then plunged forward, sure of himself and that they were both hungering for this. The heat of friction as he stroked against her inner walls ignited his lust to the point where he could not stop.

Slocum began thrusting hard, deep, fast. Claudia's legs spread wider apart as she took him; then she began kicking her feet out hard, constricting the tightness already surrounding his manhood. It felt as if he had thrust himself into a fleshy, warm, moist vise. When she began tensing and relaxing her strong inner muscles, Slocum was unable to continue with the measured strokes he had wanted.

He went wild, hips flying like a shuttlecock, driving inward as he tried to split her in half with his fleshy sword. Claudia's ankles locked behind him and kept him firmly in place. Slocum's powerful thrusts lifted her entirely from the floor, and then the world swung in a wild kaleidoscope around him. He felt the hot torrent building within, and then it surged outward in utter release.

He was dimly aware of Claudia's cries as new passion seized her in its ultimate grip. Then they sank down together, spent.

"Oh, John," she whispered hotly in his ear. "What would it be like if we were ever able to make love in a bed?"

"This is just fine," he said. But her comment sent his mind tumbling in different directions. He was owed the money. The gold was his by right of being arrested twice, being shot at, being washed down a mountain, and traipsing around the countryside and finding nothing but woe.

With the gold from the payroll robbery, he could get the finest hotel room in Denver so he and Claudia could spend as much time on that feather mattress as either could tolerate. He was owed that money. And he would get it.

"You seemed sort of distant for a moment, John. What were you thinking?"

"About you and how you'd look in a fine new dress, parading up and down around Larimer Square in Denver."

"The gold," she said. "You were thinking of the gold."

Slocum didn't answer because he didn't want to lie.

Claudia giggled like a schoolgirl. "I was thinking the same thing."

"What happened to you and Goggins when the water washed us apart?"

Slocum felt her tense and try to pull away. He held her close and she finally relented, laying her head on his shoulder.

"What an awful man. He tried to kill me."

"What?"

"I think he did, at least. I was tumbling all about, rolling down the side of the mountain, and got tangled up. That's how I tore my blouse." She displayed her tattered blouse, but all Slocum saw was the bare breast.

"What did Goggins do?"

"We were both pretty waterlogged, but I swear he tried

to hit me with a rock. He picked up a stone as big as his fist and tried to smash it into my head. He slipped on the wet ground and then fell beside me. The look in his eyes as he glared at me was so . . . evil."

"You couldn't be mistaken?"

"I don't see how. I was tangled up, but managed to grab for him when a new wall of water crashed down on us. I don't know how I thought I could save him—or why. I felt his fingers slip through mine. It was so wet. And then the water hit us like a hammer blow."

"He was washed away?"

"I never saw what happened to him. I sputtered and fought to get free, but my tangled clothing saved me from being washed farther downhill. I lost some skin—"

"Not anywhere that mattered," Slocum said, his hand resting warmly on her breast. She snuggled a little closer.

"And a lot of fabric," Claudia went on. "By the time I was able to free myself, the worst of the flood was over. It was still raining heavily, but I wasn't in any kind of danger of being swept away then."

"Where'd you go? I tried to find you at the shack, but there wasn't any trace."

"You did? I never thought of going back there. As a rendezvous? Anyway, I set out at an angle to the slope and eventually came to the canyon floor. The arroyo down the middle of the canyon was overflowing and I simply found a tree that seemed sturdy, sat down, and hugged it until the rain stopped. Even then I was afraid to move until I heard someone coming."

"Wilmer?"

"Why, yes, how'd you know?"

"He double-crossed me. Marshal Hanks came along and Wilmer saw an easy way to make a quick hundred dollars. He turned me over to the marshal."

"But you're not—he could have—oh!" Claudia was outraged when she realized what Slocum had told her. "It's a good thing I didn't reveal my hiding place then. I thought I heard horsemen. It turned out to be Neale and two of his men."

"Did you see them gun down the marshal?"

"I went back up the mountain, hiding the best I could. I heard gunfire, but that only made me run faster. Then I . . . I saw you and those horrid outlaws and the rest you know."

Slocum held Claudia closely for a while, thinking about what they could do to find the gold. Goggins trying to kill Claudia made no sense unless he knew where the gold was hidden—or thought he did. If he had uncovered the hiding place, he would have been long gone by now. Slocum pushed that matter aside. He would settle accounts with Goggins when their paths crossed again.

Right now he had to figure out how to locate the stolen payroll.

His attention was pulled away from such mental pursuits by more physical demands of a willing, wanton woman. Somehow, Slocum didn't mind at all. For the moment.

18

"What do we do, John? I . . . I can't seem to get things straight in my head." Claudia wiped at tears leaking from her eyes. Behind the violet was a map of bloodshot veins.

"I'm not giving up on getting the gold. Right now, I think I—we—deserve it for all our trouble."

"We've looked everywhere. Even if we get the painting back, what would it matter? The painting has given up all the information we can squeeze out of it. Hasn't it?"

"There might be something under the paint," Slocum suggested. He rubbed his hand against his shirt, remembering how the blue had rubbed off easily after all this time. The painting had been completed months ago and then sent to Claudia. The paint shouldn't come off as easily as it did.

"Why wouldn't Papa have told me? Or given a hint?"

"No reason," Slocum said glumly. "The one clue to all this I don't understand is Goggins' name scratched into the wall of that mineshaft. What was it supposed to mean?"

"Maybe we didn't look far enough," Claudia said. "The walls had all kinds of marks on them, but we only looked at the word."

"You might have something there," Slocum said, "but I don't know what it is." He scowled as he tried to remember what they had done when they'd found the name on the rock wall. He had lit matches and peered closely. Claudia might be right that they had missed something more, maybe higher or lower on the wall. But what could it be? Goggins had obviously not known where the payroll was hidden, or he would have been long gone and living high on the hog far away from Fort Union and the cavalry hunting for their gold.

"Goggins is probably still alive and hunting for the gold," Slocum said. "I reckon Wilmer is too. We know Neale is, and has been for some time. The marshal is dead, and several of Neale's gang have joined him in hell."

"And my sister," Claudia said, crying openly now.

Slocum didn't add that her father was probably pushing up daisies somewhere as well.

"Your pa and Goggins were connected some way. He wouldn't have carved the miner's name in the mine wall otherwise."

"Maybe he's not a miner. He could be something else, someone Papa ran into while he was looking for somewhere to hide the gold."

"Or Goggins might have been his guide. Your pa was a city man. His daughter fell in with Neale and got herself killed, but not before she gave him the stolen payroll. He hid the money, painted the map, and sent it to you because . . ." Slocum's words trailed off.

"Because he knew he was going to die," Claudia finished for him. "He might have been seriously wounded. By Neale or someone."

"By Goggins," Slocum said, shaking his head in frustration. There were too many questions they hadn't answered, but he felt they were getting close. How Goggins fit in was the keystone to this arch of treachery since he obviously was not part of the Neale gang.

"What do we do?"

"I want to be sure Marshal Hanks is dead," Slocum said.

"I doubt he escaped, but he's the only potential ally we've got out here. If he is dead, we'll know we're entirely on our own."

"That's for the best anyway," Claudia said. "He'd want the gold for himself. Or if he decided to go straight, he'd give it back to the Army." She got a strange look on her face as she dabbed at her tears. Slocum realized this was the first time that Claudia realized she was part of a big robbery. Somehow, because her father had sent her the painting, she had thought of the gold as belonging to her and her alone. By actually saying it, she finally accepted that she was as much an outlaw as Neale—or her sister and father.

Slocum went to the mouth of the cave and looked out into the twilight. They were rested, had eaten, and no time would be better to explore than nighttime. He motioned for her to bring the horses out.

"Where do you think he'll be? The marshal, I mean."

"Probably where he fell. Neale doesn't seem like the burying kind to me." Even as the words came out of his mouth, Slocum wondered where Claudia's father had bit the dust.

"John, oh, John, there!"

He jerked out of his deep thought and stared through the darkness to see a pair of glowing silver eyes. He drew the six-shooter taken from one of the dead outlaws and fired in a smooth movement. The coyote working at the marshal's body yelped, more in disappointment at being cheated out of a meal than pain, and slunk into the night. Slocum hit the ground and went to the dead lawman. Most of his belly had been ripped out by predators, but enough of his face remained to identify him. Slocum reached down and pulled his Colt Navy from the man's belt. The lawman had taken a fancy to it and probably intended to keep it. Slocum worked off the marshal's gun belt and cinched it down hard at his waist. Leroy Hanks had been thicker in the middle than Slocum, so the gun still rode low and on his right hip. Slocum was unaccustomed to carrying his six-shooter there, but he doubted he would find his holster. Better to have a six-gun at his side than crammed into his belt.

"What are you going to do with him, John?" Claudia's voice was choked.

"Cover him with rocks since I don't have anything to dig with." Slocum took twenty minutes covering the dead lawman with rocks that might thwart the likes of the coyote skulking a dozen yards away. Or it might not, if the coyote and the rest in its pack were hungry enough. Slocum doubted it mattered one way or the other to the dead marshal.

He swung into the saddle and rode off without a backward look.

"How do you do it, John? You are so . . . cold."

"Not cold," he said. "I've seen more than my share of dead men. Letting any of them matter would drive me crazy. It's better to acknowledge them, then move on and never think again on them."

"Never?"

Slocum didn't answer. He was lying through his teeth. He remembered the men he shot, mostly, but the ones who had tried to kill him were always on his mind. Men like Neale and Wilmer needed to have their miserable lives ended. He glanced over at Claudia, and added Goggins to that list for trying to clobber the woman with a rock.

"The meadow's not too far," Claudia said in a low voice. "Are we looking for Neale?"

"Not exactly, but I reckon he'll pop up eventually. I'd rather get Wilmer in my sights."

"He's like a rattler, John," Claudia said. "It's just his nature to strike at you like he did. He's no more to blame than the sidewinder would be for sinking its fangs into your leg."

"And it's my nature to chop the head off the rattler

when it tries to sink its fangs into my flesh," Slocum said. He held up his hand, cutting off her reply. Ahead he saw two shadowy patches—both moved. Then a flare of a lucifer revealed two faces. One man sucked hard and blew out a puff of smoke. The other followed suit quickly. Then only two glowing coals showed in the night to give away the sentries.

Slocum dropped to the ground and tossed the reins over to Claudia. He took a deep breath, then began sneaking up on the pair. It was easier than he expected. The two outlaws talked in low tones, more engrossed in swapping lies about women they'd had and poker pots they'd won than paying attention. Slocum got within three feet of one before either noticed him. He swung his six-shooter and smashed it into the side of the closer man's head, then cocked and fired as the second road agent went for his six-gun. It took him only seconds to make certain the first man was dead from a crushed skull. Leaving either behind him alive was akin to suicide.

Slocum was past taking chances with Neale and his gang of cutthroats.

He returned to the horses and mounted. Claudia stared at him, eyes wide.

"You killed both of them?"

"You're getting better at spotting Neale's men," he said, diverting her attention. "Let's keep riding. I don't know how many men Neale has with him, but today there are four less."

"Four men died," Claudia said. "So many over a pot of gold." She looked at him and said, "What if it doesn't even exist? What if someone else has found the gold, someone we don't know, and made off with it?"

"Your pa's not accounted for. He might have moved it."

"Then why send the map?" Claudia wailed.

"Hush up," Slocum said sharply. He drew rein and waited to see if her outcry had carried through the still mountain air and been heard by another lookout. If so, nothing was being done. The only movements Slocum heard in the dark were animals he expected to be out hunting.

As he rode, Slocum began to wonder if they shouldn't slip back to the mine and examine it more closely. Taking on Neale and his outlaws was a chore best left to another marshal and a big posse. The marshal in Taos wasn't up to it, and of the deputies he had seen in Las Vegas, none of them was likely to do much to fill Marshal Hanks's boots. But the cavalry might send a company or two up here. It hardly mattered that Fort Union was a quartermaster depot. They still had soldiers capable of tracking Neale down and bringing him to justice.

"I hear something ahead, in that grove of trees," Slocum said. Movement out of the corner of his eye drew his attention. Wilmer!

"Get down," Slocum ordered. "Keep the horses quiet."

"Wilmer? That's Wilmer, isn't it?"

"And he's going after Neale. I've got the lot of them together." Slocum was glad he had recovered his Colt. He knew its balance and how it fired. Moreover, it gave him confidence he wouldn't have had otherwise. He wasn't a superstitious man, but the six-shooter was lucky for him and had never failed when he needed it most.

Running to cross the stretch of meadow between him and the bounty hunter, Slocum came up behind Wilmer in time to see past the man into a clearing. A man grunted as he shoveled dirt like a prairie dog digging its burrow. Slocum clutched his pistol, but did not move. He was more interested in seeing what was being unearthed. His heart beat faster, and reached a point where he worried it was loud enough to alert Wilmer.

But the bounty hunter was as engrossed in the digging as Slocum was. They both knew what was likely being unearthed.

The gold.

Slocum crept closer, but Wilmer was already making his move. The bounty hunter leaped forward, his six-shooter level and ready to fire.

"Git them hands of yers up, Neale. I got the drop on you!"

The outlaw dropped his shovel and went for his six-gun, then froze when he saw that Wilmer wasn't fooling. He had him dead to rights.

"Smart, Neale, real smart. Yer worth more to me alive than dead. You got a hunnerd-dollar reward on your head."

Slocum felt his anger rising. Wilmer was going to take Neale back to Las Vegas and claim the reward again. If the deputies wouldn't give him the reward money, he'd take the outlaw on to Fort Union and collect there. He had already pocketed a hundred from Marshal Hanks, and now he was going to collect all over again for the real McCoy.

Slocum aimed his six-shooter, and was knocked to one side so hard he lost his balance. Every ache and pain he had accumulated over the past week came back to haunt him. He tried to move fast, but couldn't in time to prevent a man from stomping down on his wrist, pinning his gun hand to the ground.

"Don't even think on it," an outlaw said. "Who are—" the man's eyes widened in surprise when he got a good look at Slocum. For once, looking like the outlaw leader saved Slocum.

The shock on the outlaw's face faded as he turned and looked over his shoulder into the clearing where Wilmer held a six-gun on Neale. The shift of weight was enough for Slocum to roll a bit and kick like a mule, knocking the outlaw away from him and through heavy undergrowth. The crashing as the man flailed and yelled out in surprise warned Wilmer they weren't alone.

The bounty hunter's pistol roared twice, ending the outlaw's life.

"You keep yer distance, Neale," warned Wilmer. "How many more of them road agents are out in the woods?"

"Go to hell," Neale snarled. "There are a hundred out there. You're going to have to ride lookin' in all directions at once. You let up for an instant and they'll cut you down."

"Big talk from a prisoner," Wilmer said. "What you got in that hole? Pull the canvas bag out and let's take a look."

"It's not yours," Neale said.

"Course it ain't," Wilmer said, obviously enjoying himself. "You stole it fair and square. Well, sir, I'm gonna really put things right. That gold's goin' back to the Army, and you're gonna hang fer desertion and all manner of other crimes."

Neale started toward Wilmer, but the bounty hunter shot. Neale grunted and grabbed his leg, going to one knee. He glared at Wilmer but said nothing.

"Pull it on out. I want to see what it looks like."

Neale slipped over to the hole and began wiping the dirt off. He yanked hard and sent the bag flying. Wilmer was ready for it and sidestepped the flying sack, which hit the ground with a dull thud that warned Slocum gold wasn't inside.

Wilmer tugged and opened the drawstrings on the canvas pouch, and pulled out a handful of paper.

"Ain't nuthin' in here but greenbacks. You got the gold hid somewhere else?"

"I don't have any gold. That's all there is. That's what I been stashin' away for months."

"And you chose tonight to hightail it. You bother to tell any of yer boys?"

"All of it's yours," Neale said. "Take it." He held his leg where he'd been shot. "Just let me go. There ain't enough money in the reward to make it worth your while draggin' me off to Las Vegas."

"Don't see why I'd go there," Wilmer said. "Fort Union. That's a better place, ain't it? You done killed Marshal Hanks. Gittin' the reward outta his deputies would be like pullin' teeth. No, I think the commander at the fort's more likely to pony up money for you. Might be more 'n a hunnerd dollars too."

Neale started to shout, but Wilmer raised his pistol and aimed straight for the outlaw's face. Neale subsided. But the gang leader's action told Slocum more of the outlaws were prowling around. They just didn't know where their boss was or that he was busy stealing all they'd stolen over the past few months.

"Yep, nuthin' but scrip in here," Wilmer said, rooting around in the canvas bag like a hog going after its slop. "You been real busy. Where'd you stash the payroll money?"

Slocum tensed. If Neale wanted even a ghost of a chance at escaping his fate at the end of a rope, this was it.

"She stole it. I took that bitch in and she stole it."

"You shot her?"

"Of course I did, when I found it was gone and she wouldn't tell me what she done with it. Her old man was running around these hills. An artist or something," Neale said. "I figured he knew what she'd done with the money. Him and a guide was wanderin' 'round and I asked real nice where the gold was."

"What'd he say?" Wilmer's eagerness made Slocum's trigger finger twitch.

"He got shot up real bad, but he got away. Never did tell where he'd hid the gold," Neale said. "You got plenty of greenbacks. Take it and ride out. Otherwise, you're gonna end up like Peterson."

"How's that?"

"I busted up both his legs."

"How'd he get away from you? Oh, yeah, his guide. A galoot by the name of Goggins?" Wilmer stuffed the scrip back into the bag and slung it over his back.

"Don't know his name, but if I ever find him, I'll make him spill where the gold is. I risked my life for that payroll. Lettin' it go ain't easy for me."

"Swingin' at the end of a rope won't be anythin' too

pleasant either," Wilmer said. He moved faster than Slocum would have thought possible for any human. Wilmer took two quick steps forward and swung the heavy bag with the greenbacks in it. The thud as it landed squarely atop Neale's head echoed like gunshot. The outlaw fell to the ground, unconscious. Wilmer fell to tying him up, then grunted as he hoisted the outlaw over his shoulder and carried him to his horse. It took Wilmer a minute or two before Neale was secured belly-down over the saddle. He then slung the canvas money bag behind the outlaw, and led the horse back to the hole and peered into it, as if force of will would make the Army payroll appear.

Slocum moved to step out and get the drop on the bounty hunter. If Wilmer left with Neale, only the outlaw and his captor would ever arrive at Fort Union. The money would be hidden along the way and never mentioned to the post commander. Slocum had a score to settle with both men, but he hesitated when he had the feeling of not being alone in the dark forest.

He turned slowly and saw a shadow moving to his right. Slocum pointed his six-shooter at the phantasm, and then hesitated firing.

The ghostly form moved with surprising speed to reach the clearing.

"Hold on, you son of a bitch," the shadow called. "You're tryin' to rob me!"

Slocum wasn't sure who the man was calling out, but Wilmer answered with two quick shots. The outlaw who had stumbled on Wilmer and his boss returned fire, and then the forest came alive. Slocum heard heavy footsteps coming from all directions, and went to ground. Two outlaws rushed past him, not five feet away, without noticing him. They were too intent on Wilmer and his prisoner.

The bounty hunter fired steadily until his six-gun came up empty; then the reports became deeper, more emphatic as he began firing at the road agents with a rifle.

Neale was still out like a light, and bobbed up and down as Wilmer urged the horse into a trot. He used the horse's bulk to shield himself until he got to the far side of the clearing, then disappeared into the woods. The outlaws converged on the hole in the middle of the clearing.

"What the hell's goin' on?" demanded one.

"I think that was the bounty hunter what's been doggin' Neale's trail fer weeks," said another.

"What was in this here hole?"

"Might be he was thinkin' on killin' Neale and plantin' him here," opined a third.

The outlaws argued for several minutes before one of them took command and ordered them to their horses to chase after Wilmer and Neale. The two who had passed close to Slocum returned, again missing him in their hurry to return to their camp for their mounts. Slocum lay silently, fuming that he had let both Neale and Wilmer slip through his fingers. If the one outlaw had been a bit less attentive, things might have been different.

The thunder of hooves rattled the stillness of the forest, and slowly receded as they raced after Wilmer.

Only then did Slocum get to his feet, dust himself off, and go to the hole and peer in as the outlaws had. Even wishing on a falling star wouldn't make the gold appear in the hole. Neale had hidden loot stolen from his own men, but it didn't include the gold.

That was still missing.

Slocum felt no elation that Wilmer and Neale didn't have it. Unless there was a miracle, he never would find where Kenneth Peterson had hidden it either.

19

Slocum worked his way back through the wooded area until he got to the spot where Neale's gang had made their camp. They had cleared out in such a hurry that two cooking fires still blazed merrily. The smell of boiling coffee made Slocum's nostrils flare from the heady aroma. He looked around, waited a few minutes until he convinced himself none of the outlaws remained in the vicinity, then went to the fire, pulled the pot from the fire, and found himself a battered tin cup. He sat on a log, drinking the hot coffee, letting it revive his flagging strength and thinking hard about what to do next. The smell of burning meat caught his attention.

Hurrying to the other fire, he saw that the fleeing outlaws had abandoned a hunk of venison, and it had finally sizzled down to the point where it burned rather than cooked. Slocum didn't care. He pulled it away from its spit and gnawed on it. The charred meat tasted as good as any Delmonico steak he had ever eaten in Kansas City. He finished the coffee about the same time that the last of the venison slid smoothly down his gullet. After wiping his greasy lips with his sleeve, Slocum decided he had eaten enough for the moment. He went through what had been left behind, hunting for anything that might prove useful later in the hunt for the missing gold. The outlaws had hightailed it, probably realizing that their boss was in the hands of someone who might be at the head of a posse.

" 'The wicked flee when no man pursueth,' " Slocum said to himself quoting the proverb.

He stooped and pulled at a corner of wood frame poking from under a blanket. He grinned crookedly when he saw that the painting had been almost destroyed. Neale had scraped at the paint, sawed the corners, done everything possible to reveal any hidden map. When he had failed to find the map, he had dumped the painting at the edge of his camp and decided to rob his own men and get away with the loot he had been accumulating since he had deserted and begun his career as a road agent. Slocum held up the painting and tried to study it by starlight. As bright as the stars were, there wasn't enough for him to get a good look at what remained.

He made one final circuit of the camp, picking up some airtights of tomatoes and tossing a few rounds of ammo into the blanket, then slung it over his shoulder and left. Now and then he had to stop to orient himself by the stars. It took longer than he expected to return to where Claudia impatiently waited with their horses.

"John! You were gone so long. And the gunfire. I . . . I thought—"

"Here's a present for you," he said, swinging the painting up and handing it to her. She took it in trembling hands. Her tears glistened like diamonds in the starlight. "There's nothing to be found on it—or under the paint," Slocum said. "Neale would have found it by now if there had been."

"What happened to him?"

Slocum explained how the gang's leader had been spirited away by Wilmer, but hesitated telling her about the bag of money. He wasn't sure why, other than there was no point.

"I . . . I don't know what to do now, John. My papa wanted me to have the gold. And you said Neale had tortured him. It is so wrong to not get the gold."

"And not return it to the Army?"

"It's mine!" Claudia flared. "Ours. You deserve your share after all you've done to help. This wasn't your fight, and yet you've been the only honest one hunting for the gold."

"I can't believe your pa put those clues into the painting and onto the paintbrush for no reason. What I think happened was Neale broke his legs, but your pa wasn't shot until after he drew everything there and sent you the painting."

"He . . . he drew this with his legs all crippled? How much pain he must have been in!" Claudia started crying openly now. Slocum put his arm around her clumsily. She buried her face into his shoulder until he felt hot tears soaking his shirt.

"I'm sorry," Claudia finally said. "I shouldn't fall apart like this." She squared her shoulders and looked up into his eyes. "We have gold to find!"

"At least some of the food's left," Slocum said, poking through the wreckage of the buckboard. He took what was still intact and tossed it into the blanket with the food and ammunition he had taken from the outlaws' camp, bundled it all, and heaved it over his shoulder.

"Is there any chance of finding the gold up there?" Claudia was skeptical as she looked uphill at the mine shaft they had searched before. "I didn't find anything and Goggins didn't either."

Slocum dropped the bundle where they had pitched their camp just above the ravine. He remembered all too well how quickly the storm had come that had washed them down the other side of the mountain. Camping in the dry riverbed was too risky this time of year, in spite of the clear, blue sky and pleasantly cool breeze blowing through the canyon.

Mention of Goggins made Slocum wonder what had become of the man. He pushed it out of his mind. They had other fish to fry. He set the painting up and studied it, turning it the way he had before to align the paintbrush arrow with north. A few bits of the word hidden in the brush strokes still appeared. This was too much of a coincidence not to mean something.

"I have a lantern. It's not too badly banged up." Claudia held a lantern with the glass chimney broken to shards, but the wick remained, as did the coal oil in the reservoir. "We can use it to get a better look in the mine."

"We should get started. It'll take us most of the day to get up there."

"We can take a bedroll and spend the night, if we have to," she said.

"A bedroll? Not two bedrolls?" Slocum saw the impish grin Claudia gave him. Even if they didn't find the gold, he was sure he would find some treasure.

"Let's go. Your canteen is full, and I'm anxious to see what we missed before." She sounded more cheerful now that they were away from the meadow.

Slocum helped her up over the row of rocks lining the edge of the ravine; then they began the steep climb. They reached the mine indicated in Peterson's painting just after noon.

"Let's get in now, John," she said. Claudia was nervous and licked her lips more than called for under the circumstances. Slocum understood her anxiety. What if they found nothing?

What if they did?

"Let me light the lamp," Slocum said. As Claudia held the lamp, he applied a lucifer to the wick. It sputtered and spat sparks and then settled down to a fitful flame. He should have trimmed the wick before lighting it, but he had no inclination to remedy that now that the light slanted out and into the dark mine shaft.

They went into the mine, this time carefully examining the walls as they went. When they reached the spot where Goggins' name was written, Slocum stepped back as far as he could and cast a flickering light on the entire wall.

"There, John, see? There's more than just Goggins' name!"

Slocum heaved a deep sigh and wished they had seen what Kenneth Peterson had scratched around Goggins' name before they had gone on their wild-goose chase. Peterson had tried to warn them. Around the letters spelling out "Goggins" was scratched a large symbol that looked like a tombstone. Peering closer, letting the light catch fainter scratches, showed "RIP."

"He was trying to tell us Goggins was dangerous," Slocum said. "Deadly dangerous."

"But why do it like this?" Claudia tried to keep from crying again. "Why not just write me and let me know what was going on, what he feared, where to find the gold?"

"Might be Goggins was holding him prisoner and this was all he could do."

"Being held prisoner in this mine? Where? I don't see any place where a man could have been kept."

Slocum lowered the light and studied the floor of the mine. Rusted tracks led deeper into the mine. He followed them to a solid wall.

"Part of the roof caved in here. The mine was originally much deeper." He studied the rockfall and saw a way around it. "Hold the light." Slocum scrambled up the slab of rock blocking the way and saw a cavity above. Wiggling, scraping off skin, he flopped to the other side. Claudia held the lamp to the opening to shine some small light in for him.

"What's there, John?"

He didn't answer right away. He had found Kenneth Peterson. The man's body was unrecognizable save for the twisted legs where Neale had tortured him. Either the rockfall had trapped him to die of starvation, or Goggins had tired of trying to extract the information about the Fort Union payroll and had caused the ceiling collapse. It hardly mattered since Peterson was long dead.

"I'm looking around. There's quite a space back here," Slocum said, lying. There was hardly room to move past the body. Then he lit a lucifer and held it up. Peterson had his hand stretched out, finger pointing. Slocum followed the direction to the side wall and a curiously symmetrical triangular crack in it. He snuffed out the match and felt his way around the crack. Fingers straining, he worked out the rock. It fell heavily to the ground. He lit another lucifer and had to smile. In the hole revealed was a large leather bag that could be only one thing.

Slocum took it out, opened the drawstring, and was dazzled by the glitter of gold coins. He had discovered the stolen payroll.

He turned, looked over his shoulder at the body, and said softly, "Thanks."

He hefted the bag and returned to the hole, wondering what he should tell Claudia about her father. There would be plenty of time to tell her after he got out of the musty chamber.

"Take this," he said, pushing the gold ahead of him. He wiggled through and flopped down to the other side of the blockage. Claudia and the gold were gone.

"Claudia? Where are you?"

Slocum hurried out of the mine and stopped just outside in the bright afternoon sunlight. The woman sat on a rock, the bag open and the gold coins spilled out in a fan on the ground. She looked up, her expression indecipherable.

"You found him in there, didn't you?"

Slocum considered all the ways to answer. He knew there could be only one proper response.

"He was dead. His legs were mangled, so I reckon that answers the question what happened to your pa."

"He starved? Or would he have died of thirst?"

"There was no way he could get out. The rockfall was caused by the shoring giving way."

"He did so much to see that I knew how to get the gold. He wanted me to have the gold." Claudia looked up, her expression unreadable. Her eyes widened as she reached down into the folds of her skirt and whipped out a six-shooter.

"You don't have to—" Slocum began. He flinched when she pulled the trigger. It took him an instant to realize she had missed him. Slocum reached for his Colt, then saw her eyes were focused past him. He went into a crouch, drew his six-gun, and had it out, cocked and ready, as he spun around. There was no need to shoot. Claudia's bullet had caught Goggins in the middle of the forehead. The man had been ready to bash in Slocum's head with an ax.

"He just sort of appeared. I don't know where he was hiding. Is he dead?"

"Very," Slocum said.

Claudia got up, pushed past Slocum, and started to fire again into Goggins' dead body. He grabbed her wrist and pulled the pistol away.

"There's no need. He's as dead as he can get."

"He's responsible. He murdered my father. I know it. The cave-in might have been an accident, but he did nothing to save him."

"It cost him the gold—and his life. Let it go at that," Slocum said.

"What about Wilmer?" she asked unexpectedly. "He turned you over to the marshal when he knew you weren't Neale. Are you going to let him go?"

Slocum thought of the sack of money Wilmer had taken

along with the outlaw, then stared at Goggins. There had been enough killing.

"He'll come to the end of the trail sooner rather than later. It's not his nature to sit back and enjoy the spoils."

"Neale will hang?"

"For desertion, for stealing the payroll, for other crimes we have no idea about," Slocum assured her.

"Good."

"I want to go back into the mine. For a while," she said.

Slocum saw her gather some things from the supplies they had brought up the slope from their camp. He sat in the sunlight, rolled himself a cigarette, and finished it before going in to see what Claudia was doing. Slocum silently watched as Claudia finished drawing a tombstone on the rock entombing her father. He backed away and returned to wait for her outside. When she finally emerged, they hiked down the hill and split the gold between them. For a moment, they looked at each other; then Claudia kissed him quickly, mounted her horse, and rode away without a word.

Slocum watched her go and wondered if he should follow. He mounted his horse and somehow his trail took him in the opposite direction, but the gold made a good traveling companion even if it wouldn't keep him warm at night.

Watch for

SLOCUM AND THE VENGEFUL WIDOW

337th novel in the exciting SLOCUM series
from Jove

Coming in March!